A COWBOY OF MY OWN

Cowboy Dreamin' 8

I0520361

Sandy Sullivan

Erotic Romance

Erotic Romance

A Cowboy of My Own
Copyright © 2016 Sandy Sullivan
Print ISBN: 9781944122218

First E-book Publication: January 2016
First Print Publication: January 2016

Cover design by Dawné Dominique
Edited by Stephanie Balistreri
Proofread by Ariana Gaynor
All cover art and logo copyright © 2016 by Sandy Sullivan

Dedication

I thought long and hard about the dedication for this book.
Since this is #8 in the series, I had to dedicate it to a couple
of my new fans.
For the girl's at work who have become huge Young brothers
fans in the last few weeks.
They have devoured the first 7 books in this series so fast, I
couldn't keep up.
So this is for Mary Phillips and Ronda Rico.
Enjoy Jonathan and Mandy!

A COWBOY OF MY OWN

Cowboy Dreamin' 8

Sandy Sullivan

Chapter One

Jonathan Young glanced through his lashes at the blonde woman serving breakfast behind the counter. The pink streak in her hair always captivated him, as did her blue eyes, curvy body, and bold attitude. He liked her a lot, but what the hell to do about it.

The form fitting tank top she wore showed off her breasts to perfection but didn't give too much away. She wore low-slung jeans that hugged her hips, making his fingers tingle to touch her everywhere.

Being the shy Young brother didn't bode well for finding women. Of course, he could always take advantage of his brothers' castoffs. He didn't like to at all, but he wasn't the in your face kind of cowboy either. He did the website, advertising, and marketing for the ranch so he sat behind his computer all day messing with codes.

He sipped his coffee while he watched her interact with the guests. She'd been working in the ranch's kitchen for a couple of years now besides being good friends with several of his brothers' wives.

Mandy.

Even her name rolled off his tongue like a caress.

Laughter burst from her lips causing a shiver to skitter down his back. He wanted her. No doubt about it.

Maybe he should ask one of his brothers what to do about his attraction for the leggy blonde. Nah. Not a good idea. They would razz him beyond a tolerable level if he even thought about mentioning his fascination with her.

She captured her bottom lip between her teeth. *Damn.* He wanted to suck that pouty little piece of flesh.

When her gaze locked with his, he looked quickly at his coffee cup. He couldn't let her catch him watching her. That wouldn't do at all. She couldn't know about his desire for her, otherwise he wouldn't be able to function. He already knew she wanted him. It wasn't a secret around the ranch, but he just didn't have the balls to approach her and take things to the next level.

Damn this shyness. It was almost debilitating to him. He didn't know what to do about it. He wasn't shy around his family, just in social situations and with women. Good Lord, was he shy around women.

He'd had a few girlfriends in his life, but not many. After the one terrible breakup in high school, he tended to avoid situations where he would have to prove his manhood to anyone.

He hadn't had sex in a long time, too long. After Melissa had laughed when he tried to get her to have sex with him in high school, he'd avoided those types of situations like the plague. What he needed was to get laid.

When he looked back up, Mandy's gaze had moved on to one of the guests in front of her as she smiled.

Wow, her smile twisted his guts into knots.

This shit is for the birds. I need to stop this and just talk to her.

"Jonathan?"

"Sorry. What did you say, Mom?"

"How is the new marketing campaign coming?"

"Really good. Our website traffic has increased by over a thousand hits per month. I'm pushing for more, but it's a start."

"That's great."

"Yes and if it translates to bookings, that's even better."

His mother signaled for the family to get their plates from the serving line. As the group got to their feet to file over for breakfast, the noise of the room rose exponentially. There was a large group of romance writers at the ranch this weekend, who were friends or acquaintances of each other and the conversations going on around the room seemed to be really loud.

Mesa sat with one of the groups at another table since she knew a large portion of the attendees. Joel managed their two children while she did her best to entertain the group of writers.

It seemed most of them wrote westerns, which made it kind of amusing but expected with them being on the ranch. They said it was for research as they followed his brothers around while they did their chores. Luckily, most of them left him alone since he didn't fit their idea of the cowboy persona.

Cowboy. Why couldn't he be more like his brothers in that way? They all seemed to be naturals at the cowboy thing. Him? Not so much. Yeah, he knew how to ride, rope, handle the animals, and do all the other things cowboys did, but he would rather leave it to Joey. The youngest of the Young clan did all the wrangling with the horses, although they all took their turns with ranch work during calving season.

As he moved in front of Mandy in the serving line, he tipped his hat as she said, "Morning."

"Mornin'."

"Are you busy later?" she asked, her blue eyes taking in his entire frame in one sweep of her gaze.

"Not really."

"Okay. I wanted to ask you some questions if you have time."

"Um, sure." He dropped his gaze to his plate as he moved down the line. His stomach knotted. He would be alone with her. Damn.

He grabbed silverware from the containers on the serving counter before walking back to the family table. Eating might be a bit difficult after he'd actually had a conversation with her over the eggs and now had an *appointment* to spend at least a few minutes with her this afternoon. What she wanted to ask him, he didn't know, although she was in school for marketing and advertising from what he'd heard. Maybe it was something to do with that and not about him at all. What if he was blowing this whole thing out of proportion for no reason?

He put a bite of his eggs in his mouth as he glanced across the room to where she served the last few people before getting her own.

A little smile played on her lips as she winked.

Fuck.

The eggs lodged in his throat, throwing him into a coughing fit. Jackson pounded him between the shoulder blades.

"You okay, bro?"

"Yeah," he croaked as he coughed a couple more times. "Thanks."

"No problem." Jackson glanced to his left, leaned in, and kissed Samantha.

It was a rare time for them to be at the ranch since they hooked up. The two of them were gone a lot traveling while Samantha did her singing gigs. It had been almost a year since they'd gotten together and their wedding was planned for December.

Jonathan glanced around the table, noting all of his brothers paired up with their significant other. Jackson and

Samantha would be getting married soon. Joey didn't have a steady girl at the moment, but he was always on the prowl.

Jacob had Paige, Joel had Mesa. Joshua had Candace, Jeremiah had Callie. Jason had Peyton, and Jeff had Terri and their kids. They weren't married yet. Jonathan knew it would be soon. Jeff had finally realized how important his woman was to him when she had to leave for two weeks back in the spring for a job. Jeff had been home taking care of the kids without her and realized just what the hell his life would be like if she ever left. Ben had come down with chicken pox, giving it to his siblings in the process. Even though their mother had helped him with the kids, he'd been so frazzled by the time Terri came back, he'd popped the question to his longtime girlfriend on a beautiful spring day near the pond. Of course, she said yes and there was a wedding planned for June. Jeff wasn't wasting any time getting her to the altar. Jonathan had never laughed so hard in his life when Jeff had come up to the house dragging an itching Ben, trying to figure out what the heck was up with his son.

He really loved his family, but it wasn't easy being a Young from Thunder Ridge and one of the last single ones in the county. Good Lord! Everyone from Aunt Ann to his mother had been trying to hook him up with a woman. He already had one in mind.

After he finished his breakfast, he got to his feet and put his plate in the dirty dish bin before heading to his office to get some work done. He needed to get his new plan for marketing up to speed to get the bookings up at the ranch. Not that his parents required more money since Jeremiah had hooked them up and made them financially secure for the rest of their lives with his investments, but his goal was to make them the premiere guest ranch in the area. They had added spa services in the last year, focusing on massages and things for the ladies. They also catered weddings, were planning a rodeo this summer, and he wanted to make some more notes on what other things they could bring to the ranch to take them a step above the rest.

He sat down at this desk with a cup of coffee at his elbow and began typing away. Today, he was revamping the website for the ranch. The website coding page pulled up easily under his experienced fingers.

Tap, tap, tap.

He cocked his head to side listening for the foreign sound. There were so many ghosts inhabiting the ranch, he could hardly keep up with the goings on. The one that fascinated him the most was the old cowboy who hung out in the main ranch house and near the barns. They saw him often, but had no idea who he was. No one had really done much research on the old guy or the other ghosts on the place. When his family had bought the ranch many years ago, the ghosts had become part of the atmosphere and embraced by everyone at Thunder Ridge.

He wanted to do the research. He wanted to find out who they were. The whole thing fascinated him to the point where he went ghost hunting several times. He'd caught some sounds on recording devices and some images on camera, but nothing he could pin down. So far, he hadn't found much on the owners of the ranch previous to those his parents had bought the place from some thirty years ago.

They often heard giggling of children out in the ranch yard, the arguing of a couple upstairs in the mail lodge, and saw the cowboy hanging out on the front porch and in the big room of the house.

The sound came again. He climbed to his feet, walked to the door of his office, and glanced down the hall. No one was about. He shrugged and went back to his desk. Redesigning the website would take some time.

He cocked his head to the side when he heard the voice of the woman who took up a lot of time in his thoughts. His office wasn't far from the kitchen where she worked so he could hear her clearly. His fingers froze on the keys of his computer as he listened.

"I don't know what to do. He won't even acknowledge me."

"I know, honey. He seems indifferent to you completely," Peyton replied. "I wish I knew what to do to help you. It's been a couple of years now and you aren't any further in this relationship that you were at the beginning."

"Tell me about it."

"He doesn't talk much about himself even in a group setting with the family. He's the quiet one," Paige added.

"Maybe he's extremely shy or something? I mean, with as how in your face as the other boys are, it's must be hard being one of them."

He nodded in answer to the question she posed even though Mandy didn't know he heard every word they said.

"I can totally imagine that," Peyton said. "But come on. It's not like you've been secretive about your attraction for the guy."

"I know."

He heard the clanging of dishes as they loaded the pots and pans into the sink.

"What are you going to do about it?"

"For right this minute, nothing. I plan to go into town this evening, get rip-roaring drunk, and sleep my days off away."

"Sounds like a plan. We can get the girls together and join you. I'm sure Mesa, Terri, Callie, Candace, and Samantha could use a night out as well. These boys can get to be a bit too much to handle at times," Paige said. "We'll meet at the main house and take a couple of cars. Someone will have to be the designated drivers otherwise we'll have to get a cab."

"I'm so ready to get shitfaced drunk. I need to do something to get past this. He's driving me batshit crazy with his indifference."

Their voices faded as they moved to a different section of the kitchen. He felt like shit for putting her through this ridiculous thing. Why he couldn't just talk to her and get it over with, he didn't know.

He got up, shut the door to his office, and then sank down in his chair. He had work to do and thinking about Mandy Jenkins wasn't helping him get it done. Maybe he would find himself at The Dusty Boot later on tonight. After all, someone had to look out for the ladies of Thunder Ridge, right?

* * * *

Mandy studied herself in the bathroom mirror as she finished outlining her eyes with her makeup pencil. She wanted to look good tonight for some reason. Maybe she would get over her infatuation with Jonathan Young with another good-looking cowboy even if only for the night. Damn it, she was horny. She needed to get laid. It had been so long, she'd worn out the batteries on her dildo. Almost a year was a long time.

Her cell phone rang.

"Hello?"

"Hey," Peyton answered. "You almost ready?"

"Yeah, but since I'm already in town, why don't I meet you all at The Dusty Boot?" She fluffed her hair as she sprayed a little hairspray on it to give it more volume.

"Sounds good."

"Are the guys coming?"

"Nope. We are leaving them home with the kids, animals, and so on."

"I so need this night out. You have no idea."

"I had a feeling you were getting a bit uptight."

"I'm wound so tight, I squeak."

Peyton laughed on the other end of the line. "Get some alcohol in you and you'll loosen right up, girlfriend."

"God, I hope so." Blush brightened her cheekbones as she slid the bristles against her skin.

"See you in about half an hour at The Boot?"

"Yep, with bells on."

Thirty minutes later, she pulled her little car up to the curb of The Dusty Boot. A neon light flickered off and on over the door pointing the way to the entrance. The huge sign above the bar itself reflected the bar's logo in bright lights. The place seemed to be hopping for a Friday night, but then again, it was the best place in town to hook up, get a beer, do some dancing, and just hang out with friends. They had pool tables, dartboards, a dance floor, a band most nights, and lots of alcohol.

One of her best friends usually tended bar, but not tonight. She would be with the other ladies of Thunder Ridge drinking and having a good time. Peyton had hooked up with Jason Young some time ago, finding love in the most unexpected place with the rugged cowboy. The two of them were opposites to the core, but they made it work as one of the luckiest couples in Bandera. All the boys had lucked out with their respective women, finding love in the most unexpected place. The only two boys left unattached were Jonathan and Joey.

She'd sure hoped by now Jonathan would be hers. Lusting after the shy cowboy for a couple of years had been hard on her heart. Maybe it was time to give up and move on. A Young brother wasn't in the cards for her, she guessed.

A tear gathered in her eye before she dabbed it away. She wouldn't cry over him. After she squared her shoulders, she brushed some lipstick over her mouth as she glanced in the mirror behind her visor. Tonight was about her. She planned to get shitfaced drunk, have a good time, dance, and maybe find someone to go home with.

The visor popped back into place with a push of her fingers before she gathered her purse and opened the door.

Wolf whistles sounded behind her as she shut it.

She glanced over her shoulder. A group of cowboys stood near a jacked up Chevy.

"Hey, baby."

"Hey."

"You free tonight?"

"Maybe."

"I'll find you inside. I would love to see what's inside them jeans."

She rolled her eyes as she headed inside. Typical guy. All about the sex. Tonight, she might be onboard with that notion though.

She opened the big, heavy wooden door with a push against the panel. Country music washed over her in a heavy blanket as she glanced around the room trying to locate the group of women from Thunder Ridge. A moment later, Paige came rushing up to her, grabbed her hand, and dragged her toward the back of the bar. The girls had taken over a large, half-circular booth. Six of the women had drinks in front of them. Samantha would be their designated driver tonight since she didn't drink anymore.

"There you are!" Mesa took a drink from her glass. "I thought maybe you had backed out."

"Hell no. I'm ready to par-tay!" She slid in behind Paige as the waitress came up to the table. "Whiskey on the rocks."

"Damn girl. Hitting it hard right away?" Callie asked.

"Yep. I'm prepared to get rip-roaring drunk." She glanced at Samantha. "You're driving, right?"

"Yes. I brought the ranch van so I can take everyone home."

"Are you going to be okay?" Peyton asked her. "I mean with all this alcohol around?"

"I'm good. I'll be drinking Coke plain and if things get rough, I have my sponsor to call."

"Love my baby." Paige preened a little as they brought up her husband. "He's home with the kids, but he'll be right here if you need him, Samantha."

"I know, Paige. He's a great guy and I couldn't do this without his help."

"Jackson was okay with you coming out with us?" Mesa asked.

"He was fine with it. I'll call him if I need him, but it'll be okay, ladies. I promise. I'm fine."

"Okay," the women chorused together.

The waitress brought Mandy her whiskey. She took a couple of sips before setting it down. "I was propositioned already."

"When?" Candace asked.

"In the parking lot. A group of cowboys were whistling and carrying on. I told one of them to come find me."

"Wow." Candace took a sip of her drink.

"What? I'm the only single one here. The whole town knows you all are hooked up with a Young brother. The cowboys in this bar aren't going to touch any of you tonight."

"Some of Joel's friends are here. They'll dance with me if I want them to," Mesa added. "They know they are safe as long as they don't get too friendly."

"Where did you get your hair done, Mandy?" Candace curled a piece of her hair around her finger. "I want a streak like that."

"In San Antonio at a place on the square. They were really good and reasonable." She took another sip of her drink, already feeling the warmth spreading through her. "What color are you going to get?"

"Blue, I think. Something a little tamer than yours. I don't think Joshua would let me get hot pink."

Mandy touched the pink strip of hair she sported as she shrugged. She liked being bold and outgoing although it didn't get her much these days. Her gaze shifted around the bar, making the rounds of the tables as she swallowed the last of her whiskey until her gaze connected with the one man she didn't want to see tonight.

Jonathan Young nursed a beer at the bar and when he turned to face her, their gazes connected, sending a shockwave through her with enough heat, her nipples pulled tight under her tank top.

Chapter Two

Jonathan turned on the barstool to face the group of women in the corner as he sipped his beer. He was painfully aware of when Mandy walked into the bar to meet her friends. His whole body went on high alert the moment she'd stepped through the door. When she slid into the booth with the other women of Thunder Ridge, he'd received an eyeful of her ass as she sat down. The jeans she wore did nothing to hide the fact that her thong peeped out of the waistband as well as the purple butterfly on her lower back.

His cock hardened painfully behind the fly of his jeans. It had been way too long since he'd gotten laid.

His gaze locked with her blue one, across the bar. Boldly, he held up his beer in salute as he leaned his elbows on the bar behind him. He wouldn't let her nearness chase him out of the bar tonight. He was going to play the good Samaritan if it killed him. Tonight, he was there to make sure his sisters-in-law didn't get into any trouble and if that included Mandy, then so be it.

He might even break down and ask her to dance.

A big cowboy came in through the door and made a beeline for the table. Jonathan sat up on his barstool, prepared to jump in if need be. The guy stopped near Mandy and bent down to speak into her ear.

She glanced over the guy's shoulder to catch his gaze before she smiled, nodded, and then stood. The guy took her hand and led her out onto the dance floor.

Jonathan watched as the guy wrapped his arms around Mandy, firmly placing his hands on her jean-clad ass. Rage ripped through him. *She's mine, damn it.* No one should be handling her like that, but him. He couldn't move. He didn't want to make a scene, but watching it happen was getting him more and more pissed off.

A warm hand touched him on the shoulder. His gaze broke from Mandy as he focused on Candace. "Easy, cowboy."

"Hey, Candace."

"You know she's all about you, right?"

He turned around on the stool. "Is she? It sure doesn't look like it from here."

"Jonathan, she is so tied up in you, she can't see straight. But, honey, you are blowing it here. You can only play hard to get so long before she'll walk."

"I'm not playing hard to get."

"Could have fooled me." When the guy behind her moved, she took the stool next to him. "What's really going on?"

"I can't talk to her. You know how I am. Hell, I couldn't talk to you for a few weeks when you first came to the ranch. I just can't talk to women, especially her." He sipped his beer, looking back to where Mandy and the guy swayed to the music.

"Do you want me to help you?"

"I don't know."

"I can, you know. What if you asked her to dance?"

"I can't."

"Don't you want to be wrapped up in those arms, rather than him? Don't you want your hands on her ass?"

"Hell yeah."

"Then do it."

He shook his head and downed the rest of his beer. "I'm just here to make sure you girls are okay."

"Taking care of your brothers' women?"

"Yeah, something like that." He raised his hand to signal for another beer. He wouldn't drink more than a couple in case he needed to get into a brawl or something.

The song ended as he turned back around to watch Mandy kiss the guy before walking back to the table.

His stomach knotted. He'd bet his next paycheck she would go home with the guy. When she met his gaze across the bar, a little smirk lifted her lips. She knew he had watched, and she was playing it for all it was worth, the little minx.

He lifted his beer in silent salute before tipping the rim of the bottle to his lips and taking a long draw.

"I don't know about you two. You're all about torturing each other, I think," Candace said. "Are you into being a sadist or a masochist?"

"No, why?"

"Because you're all about the pain of keeping apart, from what I see."

"She wants a Young brother, and I'm not sure I'm the one for her."

"Why not? She likes you. She wants you."

"I'm not like my brothers. She sees what they are, how they act so bold and out there. I'm not like that at all. I'm the computer nerd."

"You are still a Young. Those genes run through your veins, brother-in-law. You can't deny your heritage."

He shrugged as he turned back toward the bar, contemplating the liquid in the brown bottle in front of him.

"You know, if you showed her half an ounce of encouragement, you would be surprised at what would come of it."

"I get tongue-tied around her. I haven't been able to say two words to her since she came to work at the ranch."

"You talked to her at breakfast."

"That was about work, not about personal stuff."

The group in the corner started to get loud. "I guess I'd better get over there. They're getting rambunctious, and I'm missing all the fun." She leaned in with her arm around his shoulders. "Relax, Jonathan. You'll be fine if you chill out and not make such a big deal of this. She's a woman who has a huge crush on you. Work with it."

"I'll try."

Candace kissed him on the cheek before shuffling back to the table. The girls were halfway to being drunk already. He could tell by how loud they were getting, laughing and shouting inappropriate things at the cowboys passing the table. Not that any of them would do anything since *everyone* in Bandera knew they belonged to the Young brothers and unless you wanted nine badass cowboys pissed off at you, you didn't mess with their women.

He glanced back over his shoulder to see Mandy sipping what looked like a glass of whiskey or something in a tumbler. *So, she's a hard liquor drinker, eh?* She laughed at something one of the other girls said, tossing back her blonde curls over her shoulder. He liked that she was individual enough to put that pink streak in her hair from root to tip. He turned back to his beer, thinking everything was okay for the moment.

"All of you are high and mighty bitches. You think you own the damned place because you've snagged a Young brother. Well, let me tell you this, you are nothing but pathetic losers willing to spread your legs for one of those boys to snag a ring on your finger."

Jonathan spun around to see who was making a ruckus loud enough he heard the words over the band. A brunette was standing toe-to-toe with Mandy.

Mandy shoved the girl by the shoulder. "You're a bitch!"

The women got right back in her face. "Look who stood up for the group and she doesn't even have a Young brother between her legs."

Mandy swung, hitting the girl in the eye, dropping her to the floor. "Take it back, bitch."

"Fuck you."

Mandy straddled the girl's hips and punched her again. "Take it back."

"Never."

After she landed another punch and the girl was out cold, the bouncers finally arrived to pull Mandy away. "You're leaving."

"She started it."

"You swung first."

Mandy held up her hands, her knuckles bleeding slightly from the brawl. "I'm here with my friends. I promise, I won't cause any more problems."

The next thing he knew, he was standing next to the bouncer's shoulder. "I'll vouch for her. She's usually not a troublemaker."

"See? And he's a Young, so you better do what he says."

He grabbed her arm and moved her behind him. "Shut up, Mandy."

With both hands on his shoulders, she leaned to the right to look at the bouncers in front of him. "He'll protect me."

He glanced over his shoulder. "I said, shut up before your mouth gets you into major trouble." When he turned back to the bouncers, the biggest one nodded.

"We'll leave her be for now, but keep an eye on her, Jonathan. If she stirs trouble again, out she goes."

"Got it." The bouncers left with the girl she'd punched under their arms, as he spun around to face her. "What got into you?" He took her hand to examine her scraped knuckles. "You shouldn't fistfight. Ladies, don't fistfight."

"This one does when it's to protect my girls."

"They weren't in any danger. Besides, I would have gotten involved should there been a need to intervene."

"I'm sorry."

"You should be." He ran his finger over the back of her hand, before glancing back up and getting trapped by her blue eyes.

"Do you realize this is the most you've talked to me in three years?" she asked, smiling like the cat who ate the canary.

I'm so screwed. His gaze dropped to her hand, and he automatically jerked his away like it burned. It did, burn that is. Her skin scorched his, bringing to mind thoughts of hot, sweaty bodies writhing on clean white sheets.

She dipped down to look into his eyes. "It's okay. You can talk to me anytime you want to."

"I'm going back to the bar."

"No. Stay. Dance with me."

"I...uh."

"You do know how to dance, right?"

"Yes."

"Two-step? You can two-step, I bet." She took his hand, dragging him out toward the dance floor.

How he ended up with her hand in his, his hand on her hip and hers on his shoulder, he wasn't sure, but there he was dancing with the woman who turned him inside out. He let the natural rhythm lead his booted feet as he tried his damnedest to unstick his tongue from the roof of his mouth.

He couldn't think of what to say that sounded witty, cool, or anything other than stupid to his ears.

"I never got into your office to talk to you today."

"No."

"Can we make some time tomorrow maybe or Monday?"

"Okay."

"You aren't very talkative, are you?"

"No."

"Why?"

He shrugged, dropping his gaze to her chest. Bad idea. She had on a tank top that showed off her curves to perfection, including the swell of her breasts. The freckled skin made his fingers itch to touch. He wanted to stroke his fingertips along the edge of her tank top to see if it was as soft as it looked.

"Jonathan?"

His gaze shot back to her face. "I don't know."

"Maybe you should have some more alcohol. That always loosens my tongue."

"I'm driving."

"Oh, right."

The song came to an end as Mandy slowly stepped back from his embrace. "Thank you for the dance."

"Sure." She didn't lean in and kiss him like she did the other guy she'd danced with.

"You should join us at the table since you are here to watch out for us."

"No, thanks. The bar is okay."

"Whatever you want to do is fine."

They separated near the table with him returning to his seat at the bar and her sitting back down with the girls.

He signaled for another drink, ordering Coke this time since he'd already had two beers. With a heavy sigh, he willed his heart rate back to normal from the pounding rhythm it had taken up the moment she put her hands on him. The moment the bartender returned with his drink, he downed about half in several gulps. His palms were slick with sweat and his brain had turned to mush while they danced. It was a wonder he didn't step on her toes. *That would have been just dandy.*

His cell phone rang. Jeff.

He answered as he moved toward the back of the bar so he could hear. "Hello?"

"Where are you?"

"At The Dusty Boot watching your women."

"Are they getting into trouble?"

"Not yet, but they're working on it. There's enough alcohol flowing to shut down some livers."

"Damn."

"They're fine, Jeff. I'll make sure they don't get into trouble."

"I hope one of them isn't drinking so they can get home safely."

"I doubt Samantha is. She's been doing so well, I don't think she'll fall off the wagon for a girls' night out." He shifted the phone to his other ear. "Although Mandy got into a fistfight already."

"Shit."

"It's okay. I handled it. It was some big mouth chick talking trash. Mandy punched her."

"That's handling it?"

"Easy, brother. Mandy doesn't belong to any of us so she can do what she wants. She was just standing up for the girls."

"If they get out of hand, call me. I'll come down."

"You take care of the kids. I got this."

"Okay. Thanks, Jonathan."

"No problem." He saw the waitress bring a round of shot glasses to their table. "I better go. They're doing shots now."

"Call me if you need me."

"I will."

"Bye."

* * * *

Mandy glanced to where Jonathan stood talking on the phone. "I need some hunky cowboy to do body shots off of." She signaled to the waitress. "Bring us a round of Patrón." The group cheered with a couple of them pounding on the table. She loved these women like they were the sisters she didn't have. She'd grown so close to them, she didn't miss not having her family close by anymore. She'd been through hell with a couple of them, and they meant the world to her.

When the waitress brought the shot glasses, each of those drinking took one. Mandy raised hers. "To all of us. May we each love our men hard, long, and with our entire soul."

"Here, here!"

They all slammed back the tequila, turning their glass upside down on the table as the potent liquid burned its way down their throats.

"You got your dance on with Jonathan there for a minute," Peyton said.

"Yes, yes, I did and it was awesome, even though he hardly said two words to me."

"He's not a talkative guy," Candace said.

"Why?"

"He's very shy, the total opposite of his brothers."

"He talks to you all the time."

"I know, but it took a lot for us to get to that point. We have something in common, websites and computer stuff."

Mandy frowned. Truth be known, she didn't have much in common with Jonathan other than she thought he was the hottest Young brother in the county and she wanted nothing more than to ride his hips into tomorrow, reverse cowgirl preferably. She needed more alcohol. With a raised hand, she signaled for more Patrón from the waitress.

"Are you sure that is such a good idea?" Samantha asked, sipping her Coke.

"I need alcohol. If ya'll don't want to join me, that's fine," Mandy replied. "Fortification is required if I'm going to trap me a Young brother tonight."

"Well, since there are only two not tied up already, I can imagine which one we are discussing here." Mesa giggled, already a little tipsy from the last shot.

Mandy glanced across the room, only to catch Joel's gaze narrowing on his wife and the group. *Well shit. We've been had.* Her gaze took in the rest of the Young brothers sipping beers as they watched their wives and girlfriends. They were all there except Jeff. Jacob, Jason, Jackson, Joel, Joshua, and Jeremiah kept an eye on the girls. She glanced to the right to catch Jonathan watching her from the bar. She knew he was there to keep an eye on all of them, but apparently his brothers wanted to make sure they were all safe and sound themselves.

Jonathan's gaze followed hers across the room to where the brothers sat in a booth.

"Damn." Paige shook her head. "We've been had. They're all here, aren't they?"

"Yep," Mandy replied. "Seems so."

"Well, I say we show them we can have a good time whether they're here or not." Paige held up her hand to the waitress. "Bring us more tequila."

"That's right!" Peyton shouted. "I'll be damned if Jason is going to keep me from having a good time with my friends. I haven't been out of the house, except for work, in a month or more."

Callie agreed and so did Candace.

Samantha shook her head. "You all are going to be so sorry tomorrow when you have hangovers from hell. Trust me, I've been there."

"Right now, I don't care if I'm puking on Jeremiah's cowboy boots on the way in the house. I'm having a good time tonight." Callie took the shot the waitress just dropped off on the table, brought it to her lips and threw the contents to the back of her throat. Her eyes watered and she coughed a couple of times before she wiped her mouth with the back of her hand, slammed the shot glass upside down on the table, and dared the rest of them to do the same with theirs. "Drink up, ladies!"

Mandy sprinkled some salt on her hand before licking it off, tossing back the shot, and then biting into a lemon wedge. She shuddered from the burn of the alcohol going down her throat. *Damn the stubborn-ass cowboy. If he doesn't want me, I'll find someone who does! There is a whole bar full of cowboys just waiting for someone like me to sidle up to for the night.* "Holy shit, that's potent."

Samantha rolled her eyes, as she looked across the bar toward where the men were sitting. She shook her head and shrugged as Mandy glanced over there too to catch the silent communication between her and Jackson. He raised his beer bottle in silent salute when she sipped her Coke. Mandy thought she had it going on. How the woman had beat alcohol and managed to salvage her career was amazing. Samantha had a pretty bad problem there for a while, from what she'd heard, but here she was hanging out with a group of women hell-bent on getting shitfaced. Kudos to her.

The two of them were so cute together. With their wedding coming up in a few months, things were a bit hectic around the ranch. The media had been camped out on the road outside the ranch for a few days now, anticipating the wedding because no one was leaking when it was supposed to be. Stupid reporters. The wedding wasn't until December. They planned it for Christmas so they could get married in front of the huge tree the Young's had in the main lodge every year. The reporters would have a long wait. Ah, the joys of being famous, she guessed. In fact, she'd bet a hundred bucks there were a few reporters hanging out in the bar tonight, hoping for Samantha to lose her battle with the bottle. Her friend was stronger than that though.

Mandy struggled to her feet. "I'm finding me a cowboy."

"You go, girl!" Every single one of the women in the group high-fived her before she stumbled slightly as she headed for a group of cowboys standing off to the left of the dance floor. She recognized a few of them as guys that worked the local ranches. She'd be damned if she'd go home alone tonight. Being the only single woman in the group from Thunder Ridge, she planned to find her a cowboy if it took her all night, more alcohol, and less clothes.

"Hey," she said, coming to stand at the left of one tall drink of water.

"Hi there."

"I'm Mandy."

"Noah." His gaze raked her from the top of her head to the tips of her cowboy boots. Appreciation reflected brightly in his eyes when they met hers again.

She stepped in front of him and put her hands on his chest, before sliding them up around his neck. "Well, Noah. How about a dance?"

"Sure, pretty lady." He glanced over her shoulder. "You aren't here with anyone?"

She shrugged her left shoulder. "A group of female friends, yes, but I'm not here with anything that looks like you, handsome."

"All right then. Let's dance." He placed his hands on her hips and began backing them toward the edge of the dance floor. "You sure are pretty."

"Thanks." He stepped on her toe. *Okay, so he's not the most graceful thing here.* "You work around here?"

"Not at the moment. Work seems to be scare."

Great. "What kind of work do you normally do?"

"Oh, this and that."

Well, shit. A dead-beat. "You got a girlfriend, Noah?"

"Uh, no."

She grabbed his left hand and brought it around to her gaze. *Fuck. A wedding ring.* "Sorry, buddy. I don't fuck with guys who belong to other women." She stepped back, turned on her heels, and headed back for the table. *What a waste of time.*

"What happened?" Peyton asked.

"Married."

"Shit."

"Yeah." She glanced back at the bar to see a dark-haired woman talking to Jonathan. *What the fuck? He can't talk to me, but he can chat it up with another woman?* "He fucking can't talk to me, but he can flirt with someone else?"

Candace laid her hand on top of Mandy's. "He can't talk to you because he's interested in you, silly. He gets tongue-tied around you."

She blew out a long breath. "What can I do to get this moving along?"

"You might have to take control."

"I need another drink." She glanced at the bar realizing the waitress was tied up serving others.

"That's it. Take control, Mandy. He needs a big nudge," Paige replied.

Mandy focused her gaze on her prey. She just might do that, take control that is. Seducing him sounded like a really good idea right now. When she climbed to her feet again, the room spun. She probably shouldn't have drunk the last round of tequila, but what the hell. Caring at this point, didn't cross her mind. She needed a man and by damn, she had the perfect one in mind. With a slow deep breath, she began to weave her way toward him and the women trying to get his attention. As she got closer, she realized the woman was talking, but Jonathan wasn't. He continued to sip his drink without really replying or focusing on the woman. "Jonathan."

His gaze focused on her. "Yes?"

"I want you to take me home."

"Home?"

"Yeah, I'm too drunk to drive."

"Uh, okay." He climbed to his feet, pushing the other woman off to the side.

"Well, I never."

"Yeah and you won't with him, babe. He's mine." She wrapped her hand through his arm and started for the door.

"Shouldn't you tell the others you're leaving?"

She shook her head. "I'm sure they've figured it out. Besides, their men will be corralling them soon to take them home, fuck the hell out of them, and be as happy as little piggys in shit."

The group yelled, hooped, and hollered as she got to the door with Jonathan on her arm. *I'm sure they understand what I'm going for here without giving them the details. Getting Jonathan between my thighs has been something I've been working on for three damned years now.* "Where are you parked?"

"Uh, to the side of the building, but let me tell my brothers I'm leaving so they keep an eye on their women."

"Sure."

Swaying with her support no longer there, she tilted her head to the side as she watched him walk toward where his brothers sat. *Damn, he's got a fine ass in those jeans.* Tight denim formed to his butt cheeks in a perfect caress of flesh. His western style, long-sleeved shirt stretched across his shoulders, making her hands tingle with the need to smooth the material across the width of his skin. The black hat on his head almost blended with his hair peeping out under the rim. The brown cowboy boots on his feet looked worn even though she knew he didn't do a lot of work around the ranch outside. He still rode a horse on occasion, shoveled shit, tossed hay, and helped with breaking the new horses sometimes. Even if he sat in front of the computer most of the day, he was still a cowboy at heart.

He returned a few moments later. "Okay, let's go." He wrapped an arm around her waist, snuggling her close to his side, and she sighed.

This is right where she wanted to be.

Chapter Three

Jonathan rested his hand on the shoulder of the pretty woman with her head on his thigh. She'd promptly given him her address to plug into his GPS before she'd dozed off. Soft snores met his ear as he smiled. When the evening had started, he sure didn't think he'd be ending it with her head in his lap, and her sound asleep.

What to do about her. Yes, the physical need for her had him tied up in knots. Candace said just go for it, but how? Easier said than done, he figured with how little they'd interacted in the past.

She was an enigma to him, and he didn't know how to change their relationship from acquaintances to lovers or whatever. Hell, he didn't even know what he truly wanted from her at this very moment. Lovers? Yes, at least that, but what else?

He pulled into the driveway at her apartment building and over to the side. As much as he didn't want to have to wake her, he didn't know which building was hers. Having her in his arms, even for a moment, was heaven. "Mandy? Darlin', wake up."

"Hmm." She rubbed her face on his thigh.

His cock jumped at the close contact of her mouth to his straining shaft. He exhaled on a rush.

"Baby, wake up. We are at your place, but I don't know which building is yours."

"Around to the right in the back. Building C," she mumbled before she put her hand on his thigh, using it to push herself upright.

He swallowed *hard.* Letting his foot off the brake, he drove around to the back of the apartments, and pulled into an unmarked spot. "Which apartment?"

"Two-forty-one. Second floor."

She started breathing through her nose in a rough and rapid fashion. "Oh God. I think I'm going to be sick."

"Hang tight. Let me open the door."

She dry heaved a couple of times before he could pop open the door and race around to open hers. The minute the door was open, puke sprayed the pavement, catching the tips of his boots in the process.

"I'm sorry, Jonathan."

"It's okay. Tequila will do that." He helped her out, moved her toward the grass, and held her hair back from her face as she threw up again. The stench of alcohol permeated the air around them, making his stomach roll too. He didn't do puke very well. He swallowed several times, willing the nausea bombarding him to settle down, as she continued to throw up everything in her stomach. "Honey, we need to get you inside," he said, after a few minutes of silence.

"Okay. My purse is in the truck. My keys are in there."

"Stay here." He grabbed her purse from the floor board, before pushing the doors shut and locking the truck. "Let's go." With her keys in hand, he helped her stand up so they could head for her place. He managed to find what looked like a house key as they approached the stairs going up to her landing. "Do you think you can climb the stairs?"

"Maybe."

Shaking his head, he handed her the purse. "Hold this." He bent down, swung her up in his arms, and started up the flight of stairs, his booted heels clicking on the concrete.

"Wow. I've never been carried like this."

"Well, it was the easiest solution."

She wrapped her arms around his neck and snuggled her head into the crook between his chin and his chest with a soft hum.

He could get used to this.

"I'm sorry I puked on your boots."

"It's okay."

When they reached the door, he slipped the key into the lock, turned the handle, and pushed it open with his boot.

She reached over and flipped the light on with her right hand.

"Thanks."

"Yep."

"Where's your bedroom?"

"Down the hall. First door on the right."

He pushed the door closed with his foot before heading down the hall to her room. He didn't have time to look over her space except to notice the cleanliness of the apartment. Everything in its place seemed to be her motto.

A soft meow met his ears as he moved into her bedroom where she'd left a soft glowing light on the bedside table. The big queen sized bed with the white comforter was home to a black, purring feline. The cat stretched out its front paws while it lifted his butt in the air and yawned.

Jonathan slowly lowered Mandy onto the bed as the cat sniffed the air before moving over to the other side and jumping down. "You need to get out of those clothes. I think you have puke on them."

"I probably do." She swung her legs over the side of the bed and sat up. "Whoa. The room is spinning."

"Too much tequila?"

"Yeah," she said, holding her head. "Can you help me?"

Oh shit. "Uh…"

"Please? I have a t-shirt I sleep in on the dresser over there." She pointed to the large dresser in the corner with the huge mirror behind it.

He could hand her the t-shirt. That wouldn't be a problem.

When he turned back around, he almost choked on his spit. She'd taken her shirt off, leaving her in nothing but a pink bra cupping her beautiful breasts. A groan escaped his lips as she climbed to her feet, unbuttoned her skirt and then shimmied out of it. Her little dance revealed a matching pink thong.

"Much better."

His heart hammered in his chest, leaving him breathless, or was that the gorgeous woman standing in front of him half-naked? Probably the latter. "Mandy?"

"What?"

"Uh…" He handed her the shirt. "Here."

"Thanks." She reached around behind her, unsnapped her bra, and let it fall to the floor. "Jonathan?"

"Yeah?"

"How come you don't like me?"

"I do. Holy shit, but I do."

"Then why don't you talk to me very much?" she asked, sliding the t-shirt over her head.

With the soft cotton material in place, he could almost breathe, almost. "I'm not really a talkative kind of guy."

"Would you do me a favor?"

"What?"

"Kiss me?"

"I don't think that's such a good idea."

"Oh, right. I have puke on my breath. Not good for kissing." She spun around, grabbed her head, and swayed a little before she caught her balance and headed for what he assumed was the bathroom to the left. "Let me brush my teeth and then we will get to the kissing part."

He was so screwed.

* * * *

The mint toothpaste tasted awful in her mouth, but it was better than the taste of throw up. Jonathan wouldn't kiss her if she tasted like puke. She really wanted to kiss him. Embarrassment at her behavior had her skin turning pink as she glanced at her reflection in the mirror above the sink. Black rimmed her eyes and her hair stuck out in several different directions. *Damn, I look like hell.* After she rinsed the toothpaste from her mouth, she grabbed a washcloth from the drawer beneath the sink, got it wet, and washed the black from her eyes. *No makeup will have to do. He'll have to think I'm gorgeous without it.*

A tapping sound reached her ears through the door. "Are you okay in there?"

"Yeah, just finishing up. I'll be right out."

She finished washing her face with a little soap and water before she shut the water off and hung up the washcloth on the rack. *Man, I look like shit.* She sighed heavily and pulled open the door to find him leaning against the doorjamb with his arms over his chest.

"Better?"

"Yeah. Sorry about that."

"It's okay." He straightened up. "You should probably go to bed."

"I know." She didn't move. The urge to thread her fingers through the hair at the base of his neck made her fingers tingle. "I hope the girls got home okay."

"I'm sure my brothers took good care of them."

"I'm sure they did." She wiped her damp face on the sleeve of her shirt. "You know, this is the most you've ever said to me."

"I know."

"Why don't you talk to me like ever?"

"Because I like you and it's hard for me to talk to women I like." He spun on his heels, heading for the door. "I should go."

"No, don't."

"I should. It's a bad idea for me to be here with you like this."

"Why?"

He turned back around to face her at the doorway. His lips were pressed in a tight line, a mere slash across his gorgeous mouth.

"Jonathan?"

"Because I want to kiss you and bury myself inside you so badly, I hurt, Mandy, and that's not good. We aren't in that kind of a relationship and being here with you is killing me."

"We could be."

"No, no we can't."

"Why not? I want you, you want me. I don't see what the problem is." She threw up her hands as she moved toward him. "Damn it! I've been chasing your ass for three years. What the hell can I do to make you see we could be good together?"

"You aren't the girl for me."

"What?"

"I'm not the right guy for you. You need someone like Joey. Yeah, maybe you should try to go out with Joey."

"I don't want Joey, I want you." She stood toe-to-toe with him. "I've wanted you from the moment I set eyes on you and that's not going to change until I get you out of my blood, however I go about doing that." She grabbed the back of his head, pulling him down so their mouths were mere inches apart as she knocked his hat to the floor behind him. "I want to taste your kiss. I want you to make love to me until we are both breathless. I want to feel you hard and pulsating inside me."

Their first kiss was meant to be magical, not hungry and passionate, but it was all about making him see that he was the perfect guy for her at the moment. Except he took possession of the kiss, and she lost all coherent thought. His hungry mouth and grasping hands came at her all at once, like he was starved for her. He forced her to accept his invading tongue as his hands wrapped around behind her, pulling her to him until her breasts were crushed to his chest. His cock strained the front of his pants as he cradled her. He was all around her.

This was a man voracious in his appetite for her body. This wasn't the Jonathan she expected.

She needed to slow things down.

She twisted her mouth from his, gasping as she dragged air into her lungs after the explosive kiss.

His lips trailed down her throat. His teeth nipped at the flesh of her neck, biting in little stinging pinches. He would devour her if she didn't stop this, but God she didn't want to stop this. She wanted this with everything inside her. "Jonathan?"

He growled.

"We need to slow down."

He halted his assault on her senses, panting hard against her flesh. After a minute or two, he stepped back, raking his fingers through his hair. "I'm sorry. That was uncalled for."

"No, no it wasn't. I forced you into that."

"I'm the man. I need to control my urges better."

"Fuck that. I want those urges. I want you to consume me, but, baby, we need to take things a little slower."

"Do you want me to make love to you or not?"

"More than anything in the world, but since I'm still half-drunk, it's probably not a good idea." *What the fuck am I saying? Back peddle here, Mandy girl.* "Don't get me wrong,

I want you to fuck me good and hard, but I want to remember it and relish it. Right now, I don't think I can."

His eyes blazed with need. She could see his pulse pounding in the hollow of his throat. He wiped his hands on the thighs of his jeans as if his palms itched to touch her. His cock strained at the fly of his jeans. She could only imagine how painful it would be to drive home and try to sleep like that. She knew what going to bed horny was like. She'd been that way for three years now, waiting and wanting this man with everything she had, but now wasn't the time. God, help her, she wanted it to be special the first time they made love.

"I, uh, I'm going to go."

"Okay." She placed her hand on his arm as he turned back toward the door. "Jonathan, this is just starting between us. Don't shut me out, okay?"

"Yeah, we'll see what happens from here."

"I'll see you tomorrow?" She glanced at the clock on the bedside table. "I guess it's today now."

"Yeah. In the morning." He reached out to touch her face. "You're a beautiful woman, Mandy."

"I'll see you at the ranch."

He walked out of her door, closing it softly behind him. A minute later, she heard the front door to her apartment close behind him.

"Tomorrow. You can bet your ass there will a tomorrow, a next day, and a next day, buddy. We aren't done by a long shot."

* * * *

Mandy groaned as she opened her eyes to the sunlight pouring through the curtains on her window. Memories flooded back as she rolled over and punched her pillow to soften the rock hard lumps irritating her pounding head.

Comfortable again, she stared up at the ceiling, picturing the night before with more clarity than she thought she would possess this morning.

Their first kiss.

His hands on her body.

Her putting a stop to his touch.

"God, what a fucking idiot I am! He would have made love to me last night, but I pushed him away!"

Petra jumped up on the bed, planting herself in the middle of Mandy's chest, purring softly.

"Hi, kitty." Mandy stroked the cat's soft fur for several minutes, her thoughts in a complete jumble. *What am I going to do now? What if he won't talk to me again? What if he doesn't want anything to do with me now?*

First things first, she needed to check on her friends after their night at the bar.

She tossed the covers back on her bed and gingerly rose to a sitting position. That's when it hit her. His smell still lingered in the room. She inhaled a deep breath, taking the scent into her lungs like a drowning man going down for the last time. Something spicy with a little hint of musk. God, she loved it.

After a moment, she realized his cologne clung to the shirt she wore. She brought the material to her nose, taking in everything about the scent she could.

Her cell rang in her purse lying on the dresser.

"Hello?"

"Hey."

"Hey, Samantha. How are the girls today?"

"Most of them are hung over and nursing headaches. The guys weren't happy when they drug them out of the bar last night shortly after you left. Most of them were so drunk, they couldn't walk. A couple of the guys just flung them over their shoulders and strolled out."

"I suppose I'm in trouble for stirring the pot?"

"Nope. They know the girls were responsible for their own behavior. I think the guys will forgive them, eventually, without too much fuss, but they'll play it for all it's worth until then. How are you doing this morning?"

"I'm okay. I need some home remedies for a hangover myself. Got anything for me from your bag of tricks?"

"Nope. Hydration is the big thing. Drink lots of water. Alka Seltzer is a good thing. It's your friend even if it tastes like shit."

"Thanks. I think I have some in the bathroom cabinet, although I'm not sure how old it is."

"Are you coming into the ranch today?"

"Yeah, I have a cowboy to corral."

"He took you home last night, didn't he?"

"Yep, and I proceeded to puke on his boots."

"Oh, not good."

"I know, but I think we made some progress last night. He actually talked to me more than yes, no, okay, and nope."

"That's a step in the right direction then."

"I agree."

"So you didn't do anything last night?"

"As far as?"

"You know, down and dirty."

"No, although he would have, I think, if I hadn't put a stop to it."

"You stopped it? What the hell for?"

"I don't know actually. I'm thinking I lost my marbles somewhere between the bar and my house before I threw up in the parking lot of my apartment complex." She shook her head, moaning softly when it hurt to move. "I want our first time to be special, I guess, and I didn't want to be half-drunk when it happened."

"Smart girl."

"Do you think so? Because I'm really questioning my sanity this morning. What the hell am I going to do if we go back to the way it was? You know, with him avoiding me and not talking to me?"

"I don't think it will. I think you made some great progress with him last night. Now that you two are over the hump, things will progress into whatever type of relationship you want."

"And what type of relationship is that?"

"Lovers, friends, fuck buddies, or whatever. You decide."

She let that sink in. What exactly did she want from Jonathan anyway? She'd been chasing his ass for so long, she'd lost track of what exactly she did want past at least one night in his arms. "I may need to take some time to figure that out."

"So be it. There isn't any rush now."

"There might be if he takes a huge step back."

"He'll come around. He wants you too."

"How do you know?"

"I've seen the way he watches you at the ranch when you aren't looking. He avoids eye contact with you whenever he can, but he watches you, nonetheless. I think it's rather cute."

"Frustrating."

"I imagine so."

"I've been waiting on that man for three years. Three fucking years!"

"Have you had sex in that time frame?"

"Yes, but not in the last year and not with anyone I wanted a repeat performance with."

"Holy shit, girl. You must be wound tighter than a spring."

"Ya think?"

"I hope you have at least a toy to take the edge off."

"Yeah, but it's not doing the trick much anymore. Every time I get close to him, I want to rip his clothes off. The bad part, now my room and my sleep shirt smell like him."

"How did that happen?"

"After I puked on his boots, he carried me to my room and laid me on my bed. He helped me get my nightshirt on and before he left when I told him we needed to slow things down, he'd been all over me."

"You are torturing yourself, you know."

"Yeah, I know, but somehow I think pushing him away last night will make it better in the long run. God, I hope so."

"I think it will." There was a pause on the line. "Listen, I need to go. Jackson walked in a second ago, and we need to talk about some scheduling stuff with concerts coming up."

"Okay. I'll talk to you later."

"Take care, honey, and don't worry. I think you did the right thing."

"Thanks, Samantha."

Once her friend hung up, Mandy grabbed some clothes and headed for the bathroom. She needed to shower before she went out to the ranch, and she hoped her day turned out the way she wanted, with Jonathan begging to make love to her before the night was through.

Chapter Four

Jonathan pushed himself away from his desk in his office, his thoughts not on work at all after the night before. After he'd pulled into the driveway of Thunder Ridge, he'd found his way to his small cabin only to be torn from the quiet of his room.

Restlessness tormented him to the point he found himself staring at his computer screen throughout the night rather than going to his lonely bed.

What the hell had happened?

He raked his fingers through his hair before tipping his head back on his shoulders to stare at the ceiling above his head. Memories of the night before tortured him with visions of Mandy as he kissed her, touched her, and fought with himself about making love to her like he wanted to. She wanted him, he knew that, but after she put the brakes on what they were about to do, he realized she was right. The first time they made love needed to be special, candlelight, soft music, everything perfect. He wanted that with her.

"Jonathan?"

"Hey, Mom."

"You're up early."

"I haven't been to bed."

"Why not?"

"I wasn't tired, I guess. I've been sitting here all night, trying to get some work done."

"Honey, you look like hell. It's Sunday. Go get some rest."

"I will after a while. Right now, I'm too restless." He climbed to his feet. "In fact, I might go ride the fences or throw some hay this morning. I can't concentrate on marketing today."

"Whatever you want to do is fine, you know that."

"I know." His mother stared at him for what seemed like a long time. "What?"

"Did something happen at the bar last night?"

"No, why?"

"The others came dragging their women home, most of them very drunk, but you didn't come home right away. I heard you drive in."

"I took Mandy home. She was too drunk to drive."

"Ah."

His mother didn't elaborate on her exclamation.

"Ah?"

"Nothing."

"Nothing happened, Mom."

"I didn't say it did."

"She was too drunk anyway. In fact, she puked on my boots."

"I hope you helped her to her apartment and all that."

"I did. She was in her room and ready for bed when I left."

His mother stepped closer. "Why does your shirt smell like her perfume?"

"I had to carry her up to her apartment. She couldn't walk up the stairs."

"Such a gentleman. I'm glad you boys were raised right."

"Thanks to you and Dad."

"Honey, that's born and bred country boy right there. That is part of who you are."

"Anyway, nothing happened."

"Nothing?"

He glanced down at his boots, glad he'd washed them off with the hose when he'd gotten home last night, to at least get the puke off. "I kissed her."

"And?"

"She wanted me to make love to her. I almost did and then she stopped things. She said she didn't want to do that kind of thing being half-drunk. I left her standing in her room, in her night clothes, drove home, and wished I'd taken a cold shower."

"I'm sure you two will work things out in the end, but for now, you should probably stay away from her."

He shook his head in disbelief. He couldn't fight the small smile playing on his mouth at his mother's words. "Don't pull that on me, Mom. You did that with several of my brothers and look where they ended up, married or in a serious relationship with the one you said to stay away from."

She grinned. "True enough, but you aren't in love with her and she's not in love with you. There is a difference in your relationship with Mandy that wasn't there with your brothers."

He thought about that for a moment. What she said was true. He wasn't in any kind of relationship with Mandy, at the moment, and he wasn't sure if that's what he wanted or not. He liked her, yeah, but did he want a future with her?

"You haven't made up your mind about her yet. I understand that."

"No, I haven't. I don't even really know her."

"Then get to know her, Jonathan. She's a nice girl, otherwise she wouldn't have been working here on the ranch for the last few years, and she wouldn't be good friends with your sisters-in-law."

"I know."

"Well then, don't give into your baser instincts yet. Date her. Take her out. Woo her before you break down and slide between the sheets with her."

He thought about his mother's words as she quietly left him in the office alone to think. He loved his mother. She gave good advice, but did she really know Mandy well enough to be able to judge her and what she wanted from a relationship?

He had some thinking to do and the best way to think was to get some physical work done. *Throwing hay it is*. They'd gotten a load in yesterday that needed to be stacked in the barn. Sounded like a good place to start. A little sweat and a lot of thinking before breakfast might clear his mind of these confusing thoughts he had about the woman. He'd lusted after her for so long, he'd begun to think his dick might fall off.

Dust floated in the sunlight dancing through the slats in the barn, when he walked through the big double doors. The smell of hay, horses, grain, and cattle reached his nose, bringing his worry and stress down several notches. Even though he didn't get out and do a lot of the physical work much, he still loved the smells and sounds of a working ranch. It was in his blood.

He took in the scents with a deep breath as he stood just inside the doors. Horses stuck their heads out of the stalls with soft nickers in greeting.

"Hey, sweetheart," he said, stopping to run his hand down the nose of one of the mares who had recently foaled. The gorgeous sorrel foal stood near his mother. He'd make a fine stud for some of their mares in a few years.

The moment he stripped off his shirt and begun moving the hay bales from point A to point B, he'd felt better. Sweat dribbled down from his temples to drip onto his chest. Muscles strained from the exertion.

After an hour of straining, backbreaking work, his mind was clearer, and his thoughts were more focused.

The moment she walked into the barn, his brain hay-wired again.

"Hey." The sweet, soft sound of her greeting sent him into a tailspin.

"Hi."

"You don't usually do this kind of work."

"No, but I needed to clear my head. Physical work does that for me." He grabbed his shirt, wiping the sweat from his neck and chest.

Her gaze followed his movements before ricocheting back to his face. "Well, um. I figured we needed to talk."

"Yeah, I think we do."

"Can you take a break?"

"Sure. Let me put my shirt on."

"Don't do that on my account. I kind of like the sweaty cowboy look on you. It's nice."

He grinned as he adjusted his cowboy hat, but slipped his shirt back on anyway before he took a seat on one of the hay bales. "Have a seat." Mandy sat down next to him, bringing her clean, sweet scent with her. He loved her smell. "So?"

"I wanted to apologize again for last night. Things kind of got out of hand."

"It's okay."

"No, no it's not, but I'm glad we are talking still and you aren't running away from me anymore."

"I'm sorry it seemed that way to you. It takes a lot for me to talk to women, any women, but when it's someone I'm attracted to, it's worse. I'm not bold, like my brothers."

"I get that. Candace told me."

"She did?"

"Yeah. It kind of pissed me off because you would talk to her just fine, but you wouldn't talk to me."

"It took a lot for me to talk to her too. We had common ground in the computer stuff and websites, though. I didn't talk to her much when she first got here because she belonged to Joshua, and I didn't want to step on toes or piss him off."

"I get that now."

"Good." He wiped his sweaty palms on his jeans. He seemed to do that a lot around her. He got to his feet, facing the stalls for a second so he could gather his thoughts. "Um. Would you like to have dinner with me tonight? You know, we could go to the diner and then maybe a movie in San Antonio?"

"Are you asking me on a date?"

He spun around quickly to face her, his face hot with the blush he knew stained his cheeks. "Yeah, I guess so. My mom said I should try to get to know you better, rather than jumping into the sack with you." He held out his hands, imploring her to understand what he meant. "Not that I don't want that too, but that's not all I want. I mean, it is, but it isn't." He yanked off his hat and ran his fingers through his sweaty hair. "I'm not doing a very good job of this." The smile on her lips made him want to kiss her senseless.

"I know what you mean, cowboy. I'd love to have dinner with you and go see a movie."

The grin he felt on his lips, made him smile bigger. He liked her. He really did. "Okay, then. Um, how about I pick you up about six? We'll go to dinner on the Riverwalk before we find a movie to see. Or you can pick a movie today some time and we can find a theater to go to?"

"Sounds good." She climbed to her feet, taking a step toward him before she framed his face with her hands and leaned in.

The brush of her lips on his sent his desire spiraling. The need to have her beneath him was almost overwhelming. He pushed his hands into her hair, cradling her head, and tilted her so he could sample her mouth better.

Last night's kiss was an awakening of passion. This one was a sampling of awareness to the feelings building between them.

Her lips softened under his as she leaned into him. A soft hum escaped her lips. He felt the touch of her tongue on his lips, begging for entrance into his mouth. When he opened his lips and touched her tongue with his, his world narrowed to only her and what she felt like in his arms. He let his hands wander down over her shoulders, down her sides, and to her hips where he let his hands cradle her, bringing her in tighter to his embrace.

The clearing of a throat brought them apart slowly. He didn't want to give up what they'd experienced in each other's arms.

When he glanced up, he saw a smile playing on his father's lips and a twinkle in his eyes. "Sorry. I didn't mean to disturb you. I was headed out to feed the horses this morning. Joey isn't feeling well."

He stepped back from Mandy as she dropped her hands back to her sides. "I need to go anyway. I want to check on the girls."

"See you tonight?"

"Yes. Six o'clock."

"Right."

He watched her turn and walk through the opening of the barn doors with a sexy sway to her hips. *She's perfect.*

"You okay, Jonathan?" his dad asked, walking toward him. "I'm sorry I interrupted."

He could feel his face flush red with embarrassment. "It's fine. It kind of happened out of the blue so, yeah." He grabbed another bale of hay and tossed it to the pile he'd made to the left, his thoughts completely on the woman who'd left him hard and wanting with nothing more than a kiss.

"I'm glad to see you and Mandy getting along. It's been a long time coming."

"Yeah?"

"Yes. She's been hot on your tail for quite a while, son, if you hadn't noticed."

"I noticed."

"They why were you waiting?"

"I guess I wasn't sure about her, you know? She's bold, brash sometimes and very pretty. Not my usual type of woman."

"Do you have a usual type? Because, I haven't seen you with very many women over the years."

"Thanks, Dad."

"Observation, son. You keep to yourself a lot. I've been worried about you." His dad dropped his gaze to the floor before it came back to meet his. "I even thought for a bit there, you might be gay."

"Me, gay? No. I like women. It just takes a lot for me to talk to them."

"You weren't having any problem communicating with Mandy when I walked in." His dad smiled knowingly. "You seemed to be very into her there."

Jonathan felt his mouth lift in a grin. "Yeah. You could say that." He turned back to the hay to move another bale. "She's a good kisser."

"I'm glad you two are hitting it off finally."

"Me too. She's been an interest of mine for quite a while."

His dad grabbed a bale of hay to toss into the stall of the horse Jonathan had stopped to pet. "So, you two are going on a date?"

"Yep. I asked her to dinner and a movie."

"Great start."

He tossed two more bales. "I thought so. I want to go slow with her. Get to know her some."

"Sounds like a good plan."

"Mom told me to stay away from her."

"Your mother has this reverse psychology thing working on you boys. She's all about daughters and grandbabies."

"I know."

James grabbed the water hose and began filling a bucket. "Works though."

"Yeah, kind of. The minute she said I should stay away from Mandy, I wanted nothing more than to find her, lay her out on one of these hay bales, and make love to her."

"Hay bales are scratchy on delicate skin."

"True, but you would know this how?"

"We didn't have nine boys without knowing how hay feels a few times, son."

"TMI, Dad."

His dad laughed as he shut the water off. "Come on now. You know how babies are made."

"True, but I don't need to know that my parents are having raunchy sex in the barn."

"Not anymore. I'll leave that to you boys and don't tell me you and your brothers haven't made use of the loft a few times over the years."

Jonathan sheepishly dropped his gaze to his boot tips. He hadn't used the loft himself but he knew his brothers had—several times even recently. "Well, that's not for me to comment on."

After he stacked the last bale, he walked toward where his dad was grabbing a shovel to clean out the stall. "I'm headed back inside to work on some marketing stuff. I'll talk to you later."

"Sure, son. Have fun tonight."

"I'm sure we will. Thanks for the talk, Dad."

"You're welcome."

Jonathan buttoned his shirt as he walked toward the main lodge, passing a group of older women sitting in some lawn chairs outside their room. "Mornin', ladies."

"Mornin'."

The bell clanged for breakfast a moment later. "Breakfast is served."

"We'll be right there, handsome. Save us a seat?"

"Certainly."

The women giggled like schoolgirls, and he had to smile. He loved talking to the older women. They always seemed to treat him like one of their own children. He tipped his cowboy hat at them before heading to the main lodge.

He detoured to his cabin to change his shirt. He couldn't go into breakfast smelling like sweat, hay, horse shit, and leather. A shower would feel wonderful right now, but he didn't have time if he wanted breakfast. Oh well, a clean shirt it was.

He pushed open his door and stopped.

A child's giggle drifted to him on the wind. The sound made him smile. He wanted kids someday, but with the right girl. Children were important to him.

He made his way inside his cabin, shutting the door behind him before he walked to the dresser by the wall. His bed took up the entire other wall in the room to accommodate his six-foot-six-inch frame. He needed every inch to be able to sleep comfortably since he was one of the tallest of the Young brothers.

When he reached into his dresser drawer, he pulled out a t-shirt, and slipped it over his head, the cotton material smooth and soft against his skin.

Before he tossed his sweaty shirt into the dirty clothes hamper, he brought it to his nose to see if he could still smell Mandy's perfume on the material. The faint scent made him smile. Even through the stench of the barn, he could still smell her. He closed his eyes, feeling the taste of her kiss on his lips. The lip-lock when they were in the barn, played over in his mind like a slow motion movie.

He slowly opened his eyes, hoping beyond hope that she was standing there in front of him, but alas, she wasn't. The whole thing was in his head. Soon. Soon he would have her in his arms again. Maybe tonight even.

* * * *

Mandy fluffed her hair as she stared at herself in the mirror. She'd taken her time to shower again for the second time today, splash some nice perfume in appropriate places, and dabbed on some light makeup to freshen up her appearance. Looking like a hussy wouldn't do. Jonathan was a down-home cowboy and she would be the wannabe cowgirl he needed if it killed her. Most girls who were real cowgirls didn't put on the thick makeup, so it was light foundation, a little blush to the cheekbones, thin eyeliner, and a nice rose colored lipstick. Her long blonde hair was curled in big ringlets, emphasizing the pink streak that ran from root to tip. Her blue eyes sparkled in the light over the sink as a smile spread across her lips. She definitely had plans for one Jonathan Young tonight and for several nights to come.

Her cell phone jingled on her nightstand. She had told the girls she had a date with Jonathan, so she wondered who it was. When she picked it up, she saw the name Peyton.

"Hey."

"Hi."

"Are you getting ready for your date?"

"Yeah."

"Where are you going?"

"Just out for dinner and a movie, I think. Nothing special."

"I hope you have a good time. Did you buy condoms?"

"Now why would I need condoms?"

Peyton laughed on the other end of the phone. "Honey, you are going out with a Young brother. If you aren't prepared, you'd better be."

Mandy rolled her eyes even though her friend couldn't see her. "You know, all of you are a bad influence on me."

"Us?"

"Yeah. You all think because you have one of the Young boys in your back pocket, we all should. What if he doesn't like me enough to want to go to bed with me?"

"Seriously? You can't really think he would turn down a good fuck if you offered, do you?"

"You make me sound so sleazy."

"I'm just saying, take advantage of the evening if the opportunity arises."

"We'll see. No promises."

"Okay. Call me when everything is said and done. I want deets."

"Yes, Mother."

Peyton made kissing sounds on the phone and then hung up. Mandy smiled as she thought about how her relationship with Peyton had evolved from the time they met.

She'd been friends with Peyton ever since her friend had shown up in Bandera sporting bruises to her body and avoiding eye contact with everyone in town. After several probing questions during a drunken binge, Mandy found out that Peyton was hiding from an abusive ex who'd beaten her over several years of their relationship. When she and Jason had been dating, her crazy ex had found her, beaten the shit out of her with a bullwhip, and almost got away with killing all three of them before Jason managed to shoot him in self-defense.

Even though she was close with all the girls at Thunder Ridge, Peyton was her best friend in the whole world and the only one to know her secret, the secret she carried in her heart hoping no one else would ever find out.

Mandy dabbed at her eyes, hoping the lone tear wouldn't ruin her makeup. She didn't need to feel pity this evening. Tonight was the beginning of something special between her and Jonathan, she hoped.

She slipped on a cute little tank top, a slimming pair of jeans, socks, and cowboy boots. A bit of hairspray and a fluff of the bangs lying across her forehead and she declared herself ready for anything that might happen with Jonathan.

The doorbell rang and then a soft knock echoed.

With a fortifying breath, she walked toward the front door to answer it. Butterflies fluttered in her stomach, her palms were sweaty, and her throat was dry. Why was she reacting this way? It wasn't like she didn't know Jonathan, but this would be their first official date. She was scared to death.

When she finally turned the knob, she was surprised to see Jonathan on the landing holding a bouquet of flowers.

"Hi."

"Hi."

He extended his hand, pushing the flowers into her chest. "These are for you."

"Thank you. They are beautiful," she said, stepping back so he could come inside the apartment while she put the flowers in some water. "Let me get a vase for these."

"Okay."

She heard the door click shut behind them as she walked into the small kitchen off to the left. It wasn't much to look at, but it was all hers and something she'd worked her ass off to keep while going to school full-time. Working at the local feed store for the last several years paid the rent, but it didn't leave much for anything else. Thank God for student loans and grants or she would never have been able to go. Graduating this year was the highlight of her life. She couldn't wait to get hired somewhere to work on websites and do marketing for all types of different businesses.

Once she got the flowers in some water and set them on the dining room table, she turned to face him, taking in his gorgeous self for a moment while he wasn't looking. Jonathan stood taller than the rest of his brothers, at probably six-foot-five or so, with broad shoulders, biceps that strained the material of his shirt, long, slim legs that looked powerful in his jeans, and black, shiny boots on his feet that matched the cowboy hat on his head. His hair curled slightly at his collar, making her fingers itch to run through it.

His gaze moved back to her face while his brown eyes narrowed slightly. "What?"

"Nothin'."

"You were staring."

"I like to look at you. You are one nice looking man, Jonathan."

A blush stole across his cheeks. "If you say so."

"I do. You can turn a few heads in this town, you know, including mine."

He dropped his gaze to the floor at their feet as he shoved his hands inside the front pockets of his jeans. "Thanks."

"Shall we go?"

"Sure," he said, coming toward her to place his hand at the small of her back and guide her toward the door.

She liked the gentlemanly behavior all the Young brothers seemed to have, but this was special since it was aimed at her. "Thank you."

"For what?" he asked as they shut the door, locked it, and walked out toward where his truck was parked.

"Being such a gentleman."

"You might not think I'm such a gentleman after the night is over."

"One can hope. A gentleman is nice, but I like a little bad boy mixed in there too, you know."

They stopped at the passenger side of his truck, and he turned her so her back was pressed against the door. The twinkle in his eyes mesmerized her as he leaned in, tilted his head, and nipped at the tender flesh of her neck where it met her collarbone.

Holy shit!

Her body erupted in goose bumps when he continued to rub his lips up the side of her neck.

"Bad boy, I can do, if that's what you want."

"Oh yeah." Her words came out in an urgent sigh. Her hands shook as she settled them on his shoulders, leaning into his body. He pressed her harder against the door, her back digging into the metal. Wetness coated her underwear, making her very aware of the magnetism of the man currently nipping at her flesh. God, she wanted him more than anything on the planet.

"We should get some food." His words were puffs of warm air against her flesh.

"Yeah, food."

With a sigh, he stepped back, taking his warmth with him. She took a couple of steps to the left so he could open her door.

When she was settled in the passenger seat of the truck, he buckled her seatbelt for her, brushed a quick kiss against her lips, and then shut the door behind him. As she watched him walk around the front of the vehicle, her heart hammered like a trapped bird inside a cage. Tonight would be *the* night. She was sure of it.

Chapter Five

Jonathan watched the gorgeous woman across from him as he picked at his food. He really wasn't all that hungry, he just wanted to watch her. This was his favorite restaurant on the River Walk of San Antonio, but everything tasted like sawdust in his mouth.

The edges of the fork disappeared between her red lips as she ate. His cock jumped behind the fly of his jeans, wishing they were wrapped around his straining flesh. He wanted that from her. Good Lord, he wanted her. The scent of her skin still lingered in his nose. The tang of her flesh still tingled on his tongue. The feel of her body beneath his hands made his fingers itch to touch her again.

He was such a goner for this girl.

"Jonathan?"

"Yeah?"

"Are you okay? You seem really quiet."

"You'll realize that's kind of the way I am, if you're around me much."

"I gathered that, but I feel like I'm talking your ear off. You don't want to hear all about me."

"Yes, I do. I want to learn all there is about you, all your secrets, your desires, your plans for the future—all of it."

She dropped her gaze to her plate and moved her chicken around with her fork.

He tilted his head slightly while he watched her. She seemed like she wanted to talk but was afraid of telling him something that might scare him off. There wasn't anything in the world she could say that would frighten him. Well murder, maybe, but yeah, nothing else he could think of. "Mandy?"

"Sorry. I was formulating what I wanted to say. I'm kind of an analytical person so I have to work things through my brain before I speak." She shoved a piece of enchilada into her mouth and chewed thoughtfully as she sat back in her chair. When her mouth was clear, she glanced at the boat going down the river for a moment, watching it slowly sluice by. "Let's see. I'm twenty-five. I've been in the area, San Antonio/Bandera for about ten years. My parents moved us here when I was fifteen. It sucked. I hated moving in high school. I didn't have a ton of friends."

"Where did you move from?"

"Minnesota."

"Wow. Minnesota to Texas. That's a switch in climate."

"Yeah. The heat killed me the first few years, but I liked not having to trek to the bus in snow that was waist deep during the winter."

"I can imagine."

"Anyway, my stepdad got a job here in San Antonio, so we moved. Being fifteen, a girl, and moving at that time in your life really was bad. I got into trouble a lot, hated my parents, hated the area, hated my life, so I rebelled. I started smoking pot, running around, sneaking out of the house, and generally being a pain in the ass to my parents in an attempt to force them to move back. It didn't work." She took another bite of her food, chewing thoughtfully before she continued. "Finally, I got into horses. They were my saving grace. I started riding barrels in the local rodeos. Got pretty good too, I would say, although never made championship material. I did place several times."

"That's great!"

She smiled. His heart stopped beating for a moment, before slamming against his ribs as it restarted with a thump.

"That was my senior year in high school. I finally adapted to the life here, and it's been pretty boring ever since. I didn't go to college right away, as I'm sure you guessed. Spent a few years working different jobs like the feed store. Working part-time there and the ranch and going to school has been tough."

"The Arlington family is an old family in these parts. They've owned that store ever since I can remember."

"They are great. I love them like they are my own family. They've bought me gifts for birthdays and Christmas over the years. I'll be sad to not work there anymore once I get my degree."

"What do you plan to do with your degree?"

"Well, it's in information technology and graphic design so I hope to build websites, working on computers, do marketing. Heck, I'm not quite sure." She pushed her plate away before sipping on her margarita. "How did you get so good at web design and marketing?"

"I went to San Antonio Art and Design school. I've always been one of those with a pencil and a piece of paper in my hands, drawing things I saw. When we started taking on guests at the ranch, I jumped right into building the website. Marketing the cowboy experience of Thunder Ridge was my way of contributing."

"How old are you?"

"I'm going on thirty now."

"Where are you in the pecking order of the boys?"

"Third to the youngest, so a middle child if there ever was one."

She laughed, the tinkling sound of her giggle made him smile. He liked when she laughed.

"I don't think of you as having middle child syndrome. You are too quiet and reserved to be wild and forcing your parents to pay attention to you."

"It's hard being just another Young brother."

After another sip of her drink, she said, "I can imagine so."

"So, do you have siblings?"

"Yes, two sisters and a brother. I'm the baby of the family. They were already gone when we moved here, so I was like an only child."

"That must have been lonely."

"I was, terribly so, which is one of the reasons I hated it here."

"Do you hate it now?"

"Not at all. I love Texas, and I love the Hill Country. Working at the ranch has been great. Being around you all, the girls, the animals, and the guests is fantastic, and I wouldn't trade it for anything in the world. I'm so glad your mom brought me into the fold."

"She's kind of like that. Taking in strays is in her blood, I think."

The look she shot him across the table screamed of contemplation. "Do you really think of me as a stray?"

He shook his head, afraid he'd insulted her with his musings. "Not at all. I'm not surprised my mother took you under her wing. That's what she does. You were part of the family before anyway, because of your association with Peyton. With you helping to find her and save her, my mother took you in as one of her daughters. She always wanted daughters anyway."

Her lips tilted up in a smile. "That she does."

"So what else is there to know about you? Are you close to your parents?"

"Sort of, I guess. I don't talk to them as much as I should."

"Do they still live in San Antonio?"

"Yes. They have a small house on the outskirts of town with a little acreage."

"A ranch?"

"No, nothing like Thunder Ridge. They have a few acres for horses and goats they raise. I think it's only about ten acres."

"That's a good start though."

"Yeah, right. How big is Thunder Ridge?"

"Several hundred acres."

"See?"

"See what?"

"You all have one of the biggest ranches in the area."

"Ranching is hard work, though, and having Thunder Ridge as a guest ranch makes even more work."

She leaned in, put her elbows on the table, and propped her chin on her hand. "What about the ghosts?"

"Ghosts?"

She tapped her fingers against his forearm a couple of times. "You know what I mean. I've seen the old cowboy a time or two, heard the kids giggling in the yard, and heard the fighting upstairs when I've filled in to clean a couple of the guest rooms after check-out. You've been there since you were born. Don't tell me you don't believe in them."

"I've seen and heard them too. The kids make me smile even though I'm sad they are trapped there."

"Why?"

"Because someday I want lots of kids. A big family like my parents did."

Her smile faded as a cloud of sadness came over her face. Her gaze reflected bitterness when she raised her eyes to his again.

"Something I said?"

"No." Her face brightened again. "We should go ghost hunting."

"Ghost hunting?"

"Yeah, you know, hang around the ranch and see what we see or hear. I would love to do some research on the place to find out who these people are. Has anyone in the family done that?"

"Not that I know of," he said, taking a sip of his beer for the first time all night. He'd totally neglected his food and drink indifference to staring at her.

Her blonde hair reflected the moonlight overhead, the pink streak giving her an air of defiance to the world around her. Her blue eyes were clear and sparkling when they looked at him. She had pink lipstick on that made him want to smudge it with his mouth. Her white gauzy top with the white tank top underneath emphasized her pert, little breasts. He was totally an ass man, so yeah, her breast size was okay with him. She wasn't a big breasts type woman, but they looked like they would fit nicely in his palms. She wasn't a thin girl. Her curves made him want to pull her in, cuddle her close, and find out where all the spots were that made her sigh with pleasure.

Soon. Real soon.

"What are you thinking about?"

"Nothing specific, why?"

"You had a little smile on your lips and you were staring at me." She bit her lower lip, taking it in between her teeth and nibbling on the pink flesh.

"All right. I confess. I was thinking about you."

"Me?" Her lips tipped up at the corners in a little smile. "What were you thinking about me?"

"How your hair shines in the moonlight. How your lips are just the right kind of kissable. How your eyes sparkle with laughter and then darken with sadness when you think about something that makes you uncomfortable." He leaned closer. "How your breasts would fit perfectly in my palms. How I want to—" He glanced from side to side for a moment. "Fuck the hell out of you."

"You do?"

"Yes, ma'am. More than anything in the world."

"Shall we skip the movie and go back to my place?" One of her eyebrows quirked up. "I mean, if you want to, that is."

"I would like nothing more than to go back to your place with you or my place. Either one."

"It might be a little embarrassing for me to be seen with you on the ranch."

"Why? It's not like we haven't been dancing around each other for the last three years."

"True, but I'd feel more comfortable at my place."

"I don't remember exactly. Do you have a four-poster bed?"

"Yeah, why?"

"No reason." His heart beat double-time in his chest thinking about all the ways he could tie her up. Spread eagle would be awesome. *Damn, I didn't bring rope. No matter, this first time should be sweet, sexy, and mind blowing.*

"Shall we go?"

He grabbed the check, slipped his credit card into the sleeve, and they both finished their drinks while they waited on the waitress. The moment she returned with the receipt and his card, he put everything away, grabbed Mandy's hand, and practically dragged her back toward the truck.

"What's your hurry, cowboy? We've got all night."

"I know. I don't know about you, but I'm really, really horny."

"Me too. It's been a bit for me. You'll have to take your time—not too much time though. I might burst into flames or something."

He slowed his walk. There was no reason to make this a hit and run. He didn't want that with her, he wanted slow, sexy, and explosive. He tucked her hand into the crook of his arm, bringing her in close contact with his side. Everything tingled where they touched. His whole body went on alert, not like it hadn't already been buzzing with sensation up until now. "I'm sorry. I'm a little excited about the prospect of making love to you."

"Me too, cowboy."

When they reached the side of his truck, he opened the passenger side door, and helped her in before shutting it behind her. As he walked around the front of the truck, he glanced to his left to catch her watching him. She ran her tongue over her lips slowly. Blood pounded in his ears and his steps faltered.

Tonight was going to be one hell of a night if he had anything to say about it.

* * * *

They drove through the night in silence back to her apartment. Her blood sang in her veins as she thought about actually making love with Jonathan tonight. She's waited so long for this, she could hardly believe it was really about to happen, in her apartment, in her bed. It would be something she could hold tight to for a long time to come, no matter what happened between them. If tonight was to be the only time they fucked, then so be it. The memory would sustain her, it might have to.

"You okay?" he asked as he pulled into her parking lot and found an empty, unmarked spot.

"Yes. Just nervously excited." She wiped her sweaty palms down the thigh of the jeans she wore. They were one of her favorite pairs since they showed off her ass to perfection.

"Me too." He shut off the truck. "Shall we?"

"Yeah," she said, reaching to open her door.

"Let me. I can be the gentleman here and get your door."

"Thanks."

He opened his side and shut the door before walking around the front of the truck to open hers. He held out his hand, palm side up waiting for her to place her trust in him that he wouldn't hurt her. God help her, she was afraid he would. He easily could as much as she wanted him, but she wouldn't think of that now. Tonight was for connecting, not thinking about what the future might hold. Tonight, she would feel without reading anything into the situation outside of two people wanting to take comfort in each other's arms.

She placed her palm in his, letting him help her from the vehicle. The warmth of his hand reassured her this was what he wanted. He wanted her. She wanted him. They would let the rest work itself out.

When he shut the door behind him, the bang of the metal door made her jump. The sound vibrated through her with finality. It was now or never. If they didn't make love tonight, they might never get around to it.

"Ready?"

"Yeah."

"Nervous?"

"Hell yeah."

"Me too."

"You are?"

"Yeah. I've wanted this for so long, I can't believe we are here, ready to take this step in our relationship."

She frowned. "Relationship?"

"Yeah. You know, like boyfriend and girlfriend kind of thing."

"Let's not jump the gun here, Jonathan. It's sex, that's it, right?"

His brows formed a weird little wrinkle between them as his mouth pulled down in a frown. "I suppose. I mean, I thought we could date at least. I'm not really into one-night stands, Mandy. Are you?"

"I don't think of this as a one-night stand either, but I didn't think we were on the verge of getting serious or anything. We only started dating tonight. It's been one date."

"I got that part, but I thought we might see where things go, you know?"

"I'm fine with seeing what lies ahead, but I'm not ready to call it a relationship."

He held up his hands. "Okay, my mistake. Sorry. I won't call it a relationship ever again. You can drive this bus."

She nodded as she slipped the key into the door. "Good."

As she pushed open the door with her right hand, she felt around with her left until she touched the light switch. With a flick of her fingers, she illuminated the small apartment.

Jonathan stepped in behind her and shut the door. She could feel the warmth of his body against her back as he moved her hair to the side and brushed his lips against her neck. Goose bumps exploded along her arms. Her body began to hum from excitement. It really was going to happen. They were actually going to make love for the first time, and she couldn't wait to feel him over her and inside of her.

"You are a very beautiful woman."

"Thanks."

"I can't wait to feel every inch of you around me, all warm, slick, and wet."

She exhaled sharply.

He took her shoulders, turning her so she faced him. He was so tall and so big, she wasn't sure how things were going to work. She barely came to his shoulder.

"You're so tall."

"Six-six."

"I'm only five-five."

"We'll make it work. Promise." His fingers reached for the front of her button down top, releasing each one slowly, to expose her skin to his touch.

When the material parted with a push of his fingers, her breath caught in her throat. The tips of his fingers brushed against her skin, causing her whole body to tingle from the touch.

"You have very soft skin." He buried his nose in the little crook behind her ear. "You smell fantastic. Flowers."

"Sweet pea."

"I love it on your skin."

"Jonathan," she breathed.

"Right here, darlin'."

The soft brush of his lips against her neck threw her into a fit of giggles. "Sorry. I'm ticklish there."

"Hmm. I'll keep that in mind."

She swept the cowboy hat off his head, tossing it onto the couch behind them. This gave her full access to his thick, dark curls. It had been a fantasy of hers for a long time, to bury her fingers in his hair and hold his head to her as he ate at her pussy like a starving man. *Soon.*

His lips danced from her collarbone in a downward motion toward her breast. She wanted to feel his mouth on there more than anything right at the moment.

He pushed her top from her shoulders and she let it drop to the floor at their feet. She'd worn a tank top beneath her blouse, but right now, she wished she hadn't. Too many clothes made for a frustrating scenario.

As he kissed his way across her chest, he worked the straps of her tank top down her arms, freeing her breasts from the confines of the top, leaving her in just her bra.

"We should take this in the bedroom."

"I want you naked."

"You're doing a pretty good job of it, cowboy, but with our height difference, this would be easier in there where we can lie down."

He bent at the waist, scooped her up in his arms, bringing her high against his chest. She let out a little squeak of surprise and then giggled as he strolled down the hall.

He pushed open the door with his booted foot and then closed it behind them the same way, before laying her softly on the queen-size bed.

The look in his eyes told her how much he wanted her. Fire blazed from the depths, igniting her body in an inferno of need. The desire she felt for this man went beyond what should be happening, but she didn't care. She'd been chasing his ass for a long time, and it was about time for him to pay up on the debt.

"You are very beautiful. Lord knows I want to bury myself deep inside your hot center."

"Sounds like a plan to me, cowboy."

He quickly shucked his clothes, leaving them in a pile on the floor before joining her on the bed. "Do you want me?" he asked, propping himself up on his elbow as his gaze raked over her.

She took in his form as he got comfortable next to her. His chest was sprinkled with dark chest hair with a nice little happy trail from his navel to the nest of curls at his groin. His cock stood long and thick against his abdomen. Her mouth watered to taste. "Hell yes."

He leaned in, raining kisses from her nose to her lips, down her chest to her left nipple before encircling the straining nub with his tongue. She pressed her breast against his mouth, loving the sensation of his lips on her aching flesh. "God, Jonathan."

The suction of his lips on the tip drove her need higher. She wanted him buried inside her. She wanted all he had to give and then some.

His hand wandered down her abdomen, skimming across the surface of her skin, headed toward the center of her need. "Please, touch me."

"We need to get rid of these clothes." He sat up, worked the fancy, bespangled belt loose from her waist and then worked on the button at the waistband of her jeans. Next came her boots and socks. The moment he had those off, he grabbed her pants at the waist, jerking them down and off her legs before tossing them across the room along with her panties. "Nice." He brought her foot up to his mouth, kissing his way up the inside of her foot and then running his tongue along the surface of her calf.

Her breath caught in her throat as he continued his journey by kissing his way toward where she needed him most. She spread her thighs, anticipating his mouth on her center, eating her pussy like a starving man.

When his mouth finally settled on her pussy, she exhaled on a rush. "Oh, God."

"Mmmm."

The vibration of his hum against her flesh was like a little bullet vibrator on her clit. If he did it again, she'd come for sure.

She could feel liquid seeping from her pussy as he lapped, sucked, and licked her flesh. Her body shook from the feelings he was evoking while he worked to bring her to a climax with his mouth. She wanted that orgasm, she needed that orgasm more than anything. It had been a long damned time since she'd had sex, too long, way too long.

"Jonathan?"

"Hmm?"

"Make me come."

"My pleasure."

He worked her pussy like a madman, until she was shaking so hard from holding back her orgasm, she thought her head would explode. Shivers raced up and down her spine.

The moment her climax hit, she felt a rush of sensation from her toes that settled in her pelvis. Her moan of satisfaction echoed in the small room as he licked and sucked the fluid gushing from her center. She'd never come so hard in her life. "Oh my God."

He pushed himself up on his arms, skimming his lips up her body in a slow crawl to reach her mouth. After he kissed her thoroughly, he moved off the bed for a moment, grabbing his pants from the floor. At her questioning look, he held up a condom from his pocket between his fingers.

"Good thinking."

"Yeah, I thought it was a good idea."

"Anticipating this happening tonight, were you?"

"No, but ever hopeful."

She could feel the silly grin spreading across her lips as she watched him climb back into the bed with her, the condom left on the bed beside him. "Should we get under the covers?"

"I'm good. I kind of want you bent over the side of the bed so I can go deep from behind."

"Sounds fun." She skimmed her hand down his chest, loving the feeling of his chest hair under her palm. The softness of the springy curls tickled a little as she continued her path down his abdomen. The trail of hair from his navel to his cock intrigued her. She's never been with a dark-haired man, much less one who had one of these.

His belly jumped from her touch, tempting her further to explore the hardness beneath her fingers. Her fingers continued their journey until she reached his hard cock lying against his belly. She encircled the head with just the tip of her finger, spreading the glistening drop of pre-cum from the little slit in the top. Her breath came out in little pants of air as she licked her lips, wanting that salty taste on her tongue.

He groaned softly, encouraging her touch.

She wrapped her hand around his length, slowly gliding her hand up and down the hard shaft. The softness of the skin against her palm felt wonderful.

"That's it, touch me. I want your hands all over me."

She laid her hand on his chest and pushed. When he sprawled back on the bed, she began kissing him from his tempting lips, over his jaw, across his chest, and then down his abdomen, following the happy little trail of hair until it reached his groin. She pushed her nose into the space between his ball sack and the base of his cock, inhaling the musty scent of his sex. The smell was intoxicating.

She ran her tongue around his balls, licking each in turn until he moaned and arched his back.

His hand fisted in her hair, guiding her mouth to where he wanted her most. The tortured groan that escaped from his lips when she took the head of his cock in her mouth, made her wet and ready.

She licked her way from the tip of his cock, down the front, flicking the veins she found with the tip of her tongue, until she reached the base. She relished the sounds coming from his throat. Every one of them made her smile against his flesh.

His hips came off the bed when she returned to take his entire length into her mouth, sucking as she went down and then running her teeth up the shaft as she came back up.

"God woman. You're gonna kill me."

"Sweet heavens, what a way to die." She continued to suck his cock until he was groaning incoherently, muttering her name in a growl that came from deep in his throat. The sound had her shivering as she moved up his chest, licking his skin as she went, until she reached his mouth.

Grabbing the condom from the bed, she tore it open with her teeth and then rolled the slippery latex over his cock, before she straddled his hips. She positioned his cock at her opening and slowly took him inside her body, loving the feel of him stretching her with his length. "Oh fuck."

"Ride me, Mandy."

She shifted her hips so she could slide his cock in and out of her body slowly. The tortured groans spilling from his lips brought a smile to hers. "So good."

He grabbed her hips in a powerful grip, lifting her, and guiding her movements in the best way to bring them both pleasure.

"Uh-uh. I control this." She clamped down on his cock with her vaginal muscles.

"Holy shit."

A giggle escaped her mouth as she placed his hands around the metal rungs of the headboard. "Keep them there. This is my party for the moment. You can have control in a minute."

His eyes glittered, reflecting the light above her head as he glanced up and caught her gaze with his own. He wanted this as much as she did, maybe more. The thought made her heart sing. She'd been lusting after him for so long, she'd almost forgotten how to be with anyone else. Now, she had him right where she wanted him, balls deep inside her pussy while she rode his hips into tomorrow.

She lifted her hips up and down, riding his length as she tossed back her head. The feel of him inside her was everything she'd hoped it be and more. Each push down, he met her halfway, thrusting up with his own pelvis at the same time, driving his cock that much deeper. "Damn, that feels good. Just right."

"You're tight."

"It's been a while since I've had sex."

"Feels like a soft glove wrapped around me, squeezing me while I slide in and out of you."

"Such a poet."

His hands slid up her abdomen until he cupped a breast in his each palm. He rubbed his thumb over her nipples, bringing them to achy little points of desire. "Ride me, cowgirl."

She spread her thighs a bit more, leaned forward, rested her hands on his chest, and began to rock her hips frontward, sliding his cock in and out of her pussy. The position brought everything into sharp focus, his cock, her pussy, the way he rubbed her nipples, and the spot he was hitting with the head of his cock deep inside her. "Fuck yeah."

"Can you come like this?"

"Almost there. Need a little more." Jonathan braced his feet on the bed and used the leverage to piston his cock with growing speed until she hung on the edge of an explosive orgasm. "Yeah, that's it. Fuck me." She exploded in a mind-numbing orgasm that had little points of light igniting behind her eyelids as she tossed her head back and screamed his name at the top of her lungs. "Jonathan!"

She collapsed on his chest, her breath coming out in rapid pants of air as she tried desperately to bring her heart rate and her breathing back to normal.

His hand stroke the back of her head, following the length of her hair down her back where it rested almost to her hips.

"Wow."

He kissed the top of her head as he continued to stroke her back.

That's when she realized, he was still hard inside of her.

"You didn't come?"

"No."

"I'm sorry." She sat up and moved to the side of his body. "Tell me what you want me to do."

"It's okay."

"No it isn't. This was for both of us, not just me." She leaned over and kissed him on the mouth, stroking his tongue with her own until he groaned softly. When she sat up again, she repeated. "Tell me what you want me to do?"

"Lean over the side of the bed on your stomach. That way our height difference shouldn't be so much of a problem."

He scooted off the bed and stood, looking around for something although she wasn't sure what. When he grabbed a pillow and threw it on the floor, she began to get some idea of what he planned.

As she positioned herself on her belly across the edge of the bed with her feet on the floor, cream dribbled from her pussy, sliding down her inner thigh. She spread her legs waiting for the moment he would plunge his entire length deep into her.

She couldn't see him behind her, but certainly felt it the moment the head of his cock pushed through her opening. "Oh God."

"Easy, girl."

His hand stroked her hair before sliding down her spine and then resting on her hip.

He pushed deeper until his entire length was buried inside her. The fullness was almost too much.

"Breathe."

She exhaled softly, ruffling the fringes of the bangs resting on her forehead as she grasped the bedspread in her tight fists.

He didn't move for a moment, waiting for her to adjust to him being so deep.

"Relax, Mandy. I won't hurt you."

"I know. It just feels so weird having you so deep. It's almost painful." She laughed a little. "You aren't a small man by any stretch of the imagination, Jonathan."

"You took me the other way, you can handle this."

"I know. I need a moment to adjust, is all."

"I won't move until you say it's okay."

She breathed in through her mouth and out through her nose, waiting for her body to adjust. *It shouldn't be this hard. He was just inside me, but this different position makes him feel huge.* She spread her thighs a little bit farther apart and titled her pelvis down into the bed.

He moaned deep from inside his chest.

Her pussy felt like it softened or something, to allow him in. The sensation was extraordinarily fabulous when he moved slightly, pushing his cock inside her a little bit farther. "Okay. I'm good."

"Thank you, God," he whispered, slowly sliding his cock out of her pussy and then back in. "You feel fantastic. Tight and wet."

"More. Faster."

He picked up the pace a little, giving her more and more of his fabulous cock with each plunge.

Soon he was pounding into her at a pace that had her pressed hard against the edge of the mattress. Her pussy quivered, taking every inch of him inside her, riding out the pleasure he created, until she was about to detonate in an explosion of sensation. "Oh God. Oh God. Oh God."

"Come for me, sweetheart. I want to feel you orgasm so hard, you almost lose consciousness."

Her orgasm rolled over her like a wave on the shore, completely out of her control, tossing her to and fro until she was so spent, she melted into the bedspread.

Jonathan roared his completion behind her, saying her name in a reverent whisper as he collapsed across her back, his nose buried in her hair.

They didn't move for several moments, until she grunted at the weight of his body and shifted. "You're kind of heavy, Jonathan."

He slid to her side and collapsed on the bed with his arm over his eyes. "Sorry."

"It's fine. I didn't need to breathe anyway and the bedspread smells pretty good from the laundry detergent I used the last time I washed it."

After a second, he laughed, a deep rumbling that came from deep in his chest before bursting to the surface of his lips. "You always make me crack up."

She moved her head so she could see him lying next to her in all his naked glory. Her gaze shifted down his chest, following his chest hair across the wide expanse to the happy trail in the sexy little line that went from his navel to his cock. When she got to that impressive length, she was surprised to see it wasn't as huge as it felt inside her in its softened state.

He peeked at her from beneath his arm. "I guess we need to get cleaned up, and I should find a trashcan for this condom."

"In the bathroom."

He rose to his feet, removed the condom from his flaccid cock before tying the end, and walked into the bathroom across the hall from her bedroom. She heard the water run for a moment or two as she lay there on the bed reliving the last few moments of their love making in her mind.

She'd never felt anything like what he'd made her body do. Her orgasms had been exceptionally explosive, so much so that she thought her head might explode with the sensations running through her. Her pussy was hot and throbbing from his lovemaking, and her heart hammered in such a rapid beat, she thought it might burst from her chest.

After a moment, she decided she needed to move, get dressed, or do something, otherwise, it might get a bit awkward when he came back into the room. She pushed herself up and turned to sit on the side of the bed while she brushed her hair out of her face. Her clothes lay in a pile on the floor with her pink underwear lying on top. With her toe, she picked up the elastic band and brought them up to her lap as she decided how they would proceed with this newfound thing going on between them.

Relationship?

She wasn't sure. Maybe.

She slipped her underwear on and grabbed her bra from the floor. *Clothing first, then think about the heavy stuff.* Keeping an eye and ear open to the sounds coming from the bathroom, she tugged her bra on and snapped it in the back. "You okay in there?"

"Yeah. I'll be right out. Just washing up a little."

"You can use the shower if you want."

"I'm good."

"You certainly are," she whispered.

"What did you say?"

"Nothing. Just talking to myself."

He laughed for a second before she heard the water turn off and he strolled through her doorway in all his naked glory. *Holy shit!* She had to touch her lips to make sure there wasn't drool rolling out of her mouth.

"What's wrong?"

"N-nothing. Why?"

"Your mouth is hanging open." He swiped his hand down his chest. "Did I leave some soap on me or something?"

"No. I'm admiring the scenery is all."

"You look pretty hot yourself, you know, sitting there in nothing but your bra and panties." He moved a step closer and cocked his head to the side. "I probably should get going."

Her gaze shot back to his. "Why?"

"I don't know. I guess I could stick around for a bit. Do you want to watch a movie or something?" He pushed his hand through his hair. "This after sex thing is a little awkward."

She dropped her gaze to the floor by his feet, not sure where to look when he was standing in front of her naked as the day he was born. "I know what you mean."

"Uh, let me put some clothes on and then we can figure out what we want to do." He moved toward where his clothing lay in a pile on the floor.

"Yeah, me too." She climbed to her feet, retrieved her pants and shirt from the floor before she slid past him into the bathroom, shutting the door behind her. With her back against the wooden panel, she inhaled a big gulp of air and then pushed it out in a sigh. *What the hell am I going to do now?*

Chapter Six

The aftershock of being with Mandy had totally turned him upside down. After she'd come out of the bathroom completely dressed, he'd felt stupid and inadequate. He'd mumbled something about needing to go home and grabbed his wallet and keys before ducking out of her door with his tail between his legs.

Today, he sat in front of his computer not really seeing anything on the screen. He hadn't eaten breakfast this morning, taking the chance to avoid meeting her gaze across the dining room. He'd felt like a teenager after his first sexual encounter with a girl he'd been lusting after. Now, he was back to not being able to talk to her.

"Damn it!"

"Jonathan?"

"In here, Mom."

Nina poked her head through the doorway. "I didn't see you at breakfast." She took a seat in the wooden chair across from his desk as she gave him a concerned look. "Are you okay, son?"

"Yeah, why?"

"Didn't you have a date with Mandy last night?"

"Yes."

She cocked her head to the side as her gaze moved over his face. He couldn't continue to meet her stare without revealing everything that happened the night before. No, he wasn't a virgin, but he felt kind of off this morning after having made love with Mandy. Why was he being so shy now? They'd had a rousing bout of sex that was off the charts, but today he felt stupid and awkward. Why couldn't he have the self-esteem his brothers had around women?

"Honey, don't worry. You are an exceptional man and any woman would be thrilled to be with you, including Mandy."

"But I'm not as outgoing and self-assured as my brothers."

"No, but you have your own attributes that are exceptional."

"Like what?" he asked, shoving back away from the desk and turning his chair to face his mother.

"You are kind, intelligent, careful with others feelings, very good looking, a gentleman if there ever was one, and you have the most amazing personality."

"Everything a mother would say."

"Why don't you ask Mandy why she is attracted to you and not your brothers?"

"For one, everyone except Joey is taken."

"Not true three years ago when she came to work here and found you. Some of the boys were not attached, yet she's always been focused on you."

"She might not be now."

"Why would you say that? Just because you probably had sex with her last night?"

"How'd you know?"

"A woman can tell these things. Besides, she's glowing rather prettily today. The kind of glow only comes from a woman well satisfied."

"This is kind of a strange conversation for me to have with my mother."

She smiled and shook her head. "I don't see why. I've raised you boys to be open and honest with me and your father. You can tell me anything, Jonathan. I hope you know that."

"I know, Mom, but it's kind of hard to talk about my sex life with you."

"Do you think I don't know about sex? You boys weren't born from a chicken, you know." She laughed and sat forward in the chair. "Your dad and I have a very active sex life even at our age and I know you boys were active pretty early in your teen years. The barn saw a lot of action for quite a while. How many times do you think I went out there only to turn around and go back into the house because of the noises coming from the hayloft?"

Heat flushed his face when he thought about the one time he'd been caught with a girl from high school in the hayloft by his father. She'd been his first experience with sex. Wild and experimenting at the tender age of fifteen, he'd taken her to the hayloft and found out just how scratchy hay can be on tender skin. It's not as romantic as people think.

"I didn't mean to embarrass you, Jonathan. I just wanted you to know you can talk to me about anything including what happened between you and Mandy. You don't have to give me details, but I get the impression you are avoiding her today."

"I am."

"Why? Was the sex not good between you?"

"It was fantastic, off the wall amazing."

"Then what might be the issue?"

"I feel awkward and stupid today. I don't know what to say to her. I kind of left in a hurry last night, and I'm afraid I've made her really mad at me."

Nina took his hand in her grasp. "Honey, she's not mad at you, but she is confused because you are avoiding her."

"I know. I'm sorry."

"Tell her that. She could stand to see one of your smiles right now. She's feeling pretty used."

"Ah hell. I didn't want that to happen."

She brought him to his feet, turned him toward the door, and pushed him out in the hall. "Go talk to her."

"Is everyone gone?"

"Yes. The guests have dispersed elsewhere and your brothers and their families have headed off to do their own thing. I'm going to work on reservations for the coming week."

She turned the opposite direction he was headed and disappeared into her office, leaving him standing in the hall with his hands in his pockets unsure of what to do or what to say. He took a couple of steps forward, feeling resolve stiffen his spine. He needed to apologize if nothing else.

When he turned the corner of the hall that led out into the dining room area, he saw her cleaning off one of the tables. With hesitant steps, he made his way toward her. "Mandy?"

She spun around, her eyes wide. "Oh. You scared me."

"Sorry. I didn't mean to startle you." He dropped his gaze to the floor. "I wanted to apologize."

"For what?"

"For taking off so quickly last night. I shouldn't have done that. I'm sure it made you feel kind of used and that was not my intention."

She took a seat on the bench across the table while he slid onto the other one. "It's fine. I know you were feeling kind of weirded out by the whole thing."

"Yeah, but that's not why I left."

"Why did you then?"

"You were backpedaling on the relationship thing earlier so I was afraid I'd moved too fast."

She dropped her gaze to her hands clasped around the towel she'd been using to wipe the tables with. "Listen, I'm not sure about a relationship between us. We can take things slow though, and see where they go, if that's okay with you?"

"Sure. I guess."

"I just don't know where my life is going at the moment, and I'm afraid to become too attached to someone. What if, after I graduate from my college courses, I get a job in

Houston? I might have to move. I don't want to pressure someone I care about to move with me and give up everything they've ever known."

"I see."

She reached across the table and laid her hand on his. "Not that what happened last night wasn't great, because it was. Fantastic even, but I need to take this slow, Jonathan. Can you understand that?"

"I'm at a bit of a loss here, Mandy. You've been chasing me for years and now you want to slow down?"

"I'm afraid."

"Of what?"

"I'm not sure, but I think I'm a bit scared that this relationship won't live up to the fantasies and expectations of what I've dreamed about this whole time. Does that make sense?"

He shoved his fingers through his hair before settling his hat back on his head. He didn't know what to do with her confession. Wanting her wasn't a problem. He'd been doing that for a long time now, but what if it was like she said and didn't live up to the expectations they had placed on it? They were good together in bed. That much he knew from the night before. A sigh escaped his lips as he tipped his head back and stared at the wooden beams above him. When he gathered his thoughts a bit, he caught her gaze with his. "Okay. Let's take this slow. We'll date, spend time together, and do everything couples do, but we won't talk about the future or what that might hold. We'll see how things play out."

The smile spreading across her lips made his heart skip a beat. She really was the prettiest thing he'd seen in a long time and he couldn't wait to taste her again.

"Deal."

* * * *

Mandy scrubbed the pot beneath the water as her mind wandered to Jonathan. He seemed so sad earlier when she talked about slowing things down between them. Her stomach cramped at the thought of walking away from him. She sure didn't want to, but what if he didn't understand her secret? She wasn't sure she could tell him now or ever and with all the Young family having kids, she felt left out.

Peyton came in through the double doors into the kitchen. "Hey."

"Hi."

"You okay?"

"Yeah, why?"

"You were very quiet at lunch and dinner too. It's not like you."

"Sorry. I've got some stuff on my mind."

"Jonathan?" Peyton asked, stealing a cookie from the dish on the counter then popping it into her mouth.

"Yep." She continue to scrub the same dish until she realized she'd better pull her shit together or she would be there all night washing supper dishes. After she slipped the plate under the cool water to rinse it, she put it in the drying rack on the opposite countertop.

"What happened last night with your date?"

"Not much."

"I find that hard to believe. You had the look of a very satisfied woman this morning at breakfast. Did you have sex?"

"Yeah, and it was pretty awesome."

Peyton took another bite of her cookie as she scooted her butt up on the countertop. "So what's the problem?"

"I told him earlier that I wanted to slow things down."

"That doesn't sound like you after the way you've been trying to get his attention for so long."

"I know." She grabbed a pot from the counter and dunked it in the water. "What if he finds out my secret?"

"If you care about him, you'll have to tell him eventually, Mandy."

"I can't. He wants kids, lots of kids." She turned toward Peyton, her hands full of suds. "He wouldn't understand."

"Honey, it was your fault. You were only fifteen."

"What if we fall in love? What if he wants to marry me? What then? How will I explain that I had a baby at fifteen, gave her up for adoption, and the pregnancy did so much damage to my insides that I can't have anymore? How the hell do I tell a man like him I can't have any more children?"

"There is always adoption."

"How ironic would that be? I gave up the only biological child I can ever have and then end up adopting someone else's child." Tears pricked her eyes as she fought not to cry. He wouldn't understand. His family wouldn't understand. Nina wanted lots of grandchildren. She talked so lovingly about the ones she had now that she would never accept Mandy into the fold if she knew she wouldn't be able to give her more.

Peyton hopped down and folded Mandy into an embrace. "Don't cry. You don't know how Jonathan would react to your news."

"Yes, I do. He already told me he wanted lots of kids like his parents."

"Don't judge him before he has a chance, Mandy. That's not fair to him."

"I should just cut this off right now. Walk away before I get any more attached or God forbid he falls in love with me."

"Mandy, listen to yourself. You're willing to walk away from one of the best things to ever happen to you because of some idea you have in your brain? Jonathan isn't that shallow. If he falls in love with you, then he'll be in love with you, not your ability to have children or not. Do you think Jason would walk away from me if for some reason I couldn't conceive?"

"Are you trying?"

"Maybe."

"You need a baby, Peyton."

"I haven't decided yet if I'm going to go along with the idea of having one right now. We're still newlyweds."

"Newlyweds, hell. You've been married for a few years now. It's time to start a family."

"I like having him all to myself, you know." She glanced away.

"What is it, Peyton?" Mandy asked, not liking the look in her friend's eyes. She took Peyton's hand in hers. "You can tell me."

"Jason wants a baby. I'm not sure if I do."

"You don't want children?"

Peyton shrugged as she dropped her gaze to the floor.

"Talk to me. We've been friends a long time. You know I won't say anything to anyone if you don't want me to."

Peyton walked to the opposite countertop and began to fiddle with the spices in the rack. Mandy let her keep her silence for now. She didn't want to push Peyton, but she had a feeling her friend needed to talk.

"I love Jason with all my heart."

"But?"

"I don't know if I want children."

"None at all?"

"No."

"Have you talked to him?"

"Yeah." She shrugged. "Well sort of."

"What do you mean?"

"We've talked. He wants kids."

"You two didn't discuss this before you got married?"

"We did or I thought we did, but I guess not." She cringed. "After everything with my ex and what happened, I knew I loved Jason and would do anything for him. Now that we've been together for a few years, I'm thinking there are some differences in our relationship we should have explored before we said I do."

Mandy drew Peyton into a big hug. "Oh Peyton. You need to have a heart-to-heart talk with your husband."

"I know, but I'm scared I'll lose him if I tell him I don't want kids."

"Are you sure you don't want any at all or just not right now?"

"I don't want any, Mandy."

"Oh honey. I'm sorry." She hugged Peyton to her, realizing her problem was probably a lot less of an issue than Peyton's. With the Young brothers, you just didn't tell one of them you didn't want to have children. "Things will work out. You'll see."

"I hope so. I can't lose him. My life would be over if I did."

"Aren't we a pair?"

"Right?" Peyton let out a dry laugh and stepped back. "You want kids and can't have anymore, and I don't want any and probably wouldn't have any trouble having one."

"It'll be okay. We'll get through this."

"I know. Thanks for listening. This isn't why I came in here. I wanted to help you and in the meantime you helped me."

"That's what I'm here for, sister dear."

"You are like a sister to me too. I don't know what I would do without you."

"You'd be miserable." Mandy laughed as she walked back to the sink. "Now let me get my work done so I can go home, get a pint of ice cream, and sit in front of the television to watch some lame program on it."

"Okay. See you tomorrow?"

"Yep. I'll be here."

"Night, Mandy."

"Night, Peyton." Mandy watched as Peyton went through the double doors out into the main dining area. The door swung shut behind her, leaving Mandy alone in the kitchen with her thoughts.

The night before flashed back to her in sharp clarity. Making love with Jonathan had been like a dream come true, one she'd fantasized about for the last few years, and it had been even better in person than in her dreams.

They had come to an agreement to take things slow earlier. It felt weird to think that after all she'd been through to get his attention. Why was she so terrified to think of them having a future together? Her past would haunt her for the rest of her life, but she couldn't let that stop her from finding love with the man of her dreams, right? Maybe she should talk to Nina and see what her take is on a daughter who couldn't have any children. Of course, it wouldn't matter what Nina wanted if Jonathan was determined to have a bunch of kids.

Their relationship, or whatever you wanted to call it, was too new to worry about these things. If things were meant to be between her and Jonathan, then they would work out just fine and he wouldn't leave her in the dust when he found out she couldn't give him biological children.

She exhaled sharply as determination stiffened her spine. Enough.

Things would work out as they were meant to. She had to believe that and go forward with everything, otherwise she would probably spend the rest of her life alone. That wasn't a very good option in her opinion.

She finished the dishes, putting everything in its place for the morning. After a quick sweep of the room to make sure she hadn't forgotten anything, she grabbed her purse from the desk in the corner, flipped off the light switch plunging everything into darkness, and headed toward the main lodge.

A few guests were sitting chatting quietly on the leather sofas near the dark fireplace.

"Can I get you anything else before I leave?"

The two turned to the sound of her voice, smiling as they replied, "No, thank you. You all have been very gracious with your time and energy. We'll be fine tonight." The woman raised her wine glass, showing off the deep burgundy of the liquid. "We are going to finish this glass of wine and head off to bed. We have a ride scheduled for early in the morning, so we need to be up with the sun. We are planning to watch the sunrise over the hills."

"Sounds beautiful. The sunrises are gorgeous here this time of year." Mandy slung her purse over her shoulder and headed for the door. "Enjoy your evening, and I will see you at breakfast."

"Thank you. See you then."

Mandy walked through the heavy wood door, letting it bang softly behind her as she walked through the pitch-blackness toward where she'd left her car. Small external lights lit the walkway, but other than that, there was nothing to mar the beauty of the night. Stars twinkled above her as she glanced up. The moon reflected brightly to her right, lighting her walk.

When she reached her car, she heard the faint giggles of children on the breeze. A smile lifted the corners of her mouth. The children in the yard always made her feel better.

One day she hoped to find her biological daughter again and let her know it wasn't that she didn't love her and want her when she was born, it was the fact that she couldn't take care of a baby at fifteen. Her parents had forced her to give the child up for adoption at birth. They were pretty strict Christians and didn't believe in abortion. Not that she would have chosen to take care of her situation like that anyway, but when the day had come for her to give birth, they never even let her hold her daughter, just took her away, gave her to her new parents, and never spoke of it again.

Someday, baby girl, I will find you.

Chapter Seven

Jonathan let out a sharp exhale as he stared at the apartment complex where Mandy lived. The building itself wasn't much to look at, two stories with stairs that ran up the middle and then split off to each apartment. The whole thing was a dull brown color without very much in the way of shrubbery. If it was his, he would have flowering bushes, green shrubs, and perennial flowering plants all over. Something to brighten up the place would have been nice. It wasn't very homey.

He worried his lips with his teeth, unsure of himself now. He contemplated going home, but that would make him an asshole. He might be shy and introverted, but those traits didn't make him an asshole unless he pulled something stupid. After a moment, he popped the door of his truck open so he could walk up to her place. When he'd asked Mandy this morning if she wanted to go out to dinner and a movie tonight, she'd said yes. She even smiled, which was good. He'd been afraid he'd totally fucked everything up with his behavior the other night. When she'd said she wanted to slow things down, his stomach had knotted something fierce.

A light shown in her apartment, indicating that she was indeed home. Good. Well, sort of good. That meant she really did want to go with him somewhere, at least that's what he hoped it meant.

He stopped in front of her door with his hand raised to knock, hesitating a moment as he listened to the sounds coming from behind the door. She had some country music turned up pretty loud, and he had to smile when he recognized Jackson's wife Samantha's voice as Mandy sang along.

Mandy couldn't sing very well. He gave her points for trying, though. He couldn't really say anything since he couldn't sing worth beans either. Now, give him a good two-stepping song and he'd be all over that shit.

The plan for tonight would include dancing after they had dinner. He would love to hold her in his arms as they slow danced to a good tune.

A quick rap on the door with his knuckles brought the music back down to a low hum. She opened the door decked out in a really pretty pink dress with something sparkly on the material. Her shoulders wear bare as the material of the dress clung to her breasts in some sort of silky wrap around her body. The hem reached mid-thigh as his gaze wandered down her body. *Holy shit, that's sexy.* The heels she had on her feet were open-toed and she'd painted her toenails bright pink to match her dress.

"You like?"

"Very much so. You look gorgeous."

"Thank you, kind sir." She stepped closer bringing their bodies to where they almost touched as she went up on her toes and left a brief kiss on his lips. "I'm glad you approve."

Her scent sent him reeling straight into a raging hard-on. His hands automatically reached for her shoulders to bring her in closer, but she stepped back out of his reach with a saucy little smile on her lips, one that made him want to toss her over his shoulder and head straight into her bedroom.

"Uh-uh. We have reservations somewhere, right?"

"Yeah."

"Let me grab my wrap then and we'll go."

"Tease."

"You bet, cowboy."

Her curls bounced on her shoulders as she walked into the other room. He enjoyed the view of her going almost as much as the one of her coming back toward him. "Ready?"

He cleared his throat as a small squeak came out from between his lips. "Yeah. Let's go before I do something I might regret later."

"No regrets, Jonathan."

"You say that now, but if I slammed the door and took you right there on your table, you'd probably regret it."

"Oh, hell no, I wouldn't, but we do already have plans." She touched his lips with her fingertip. "Keep that in mind for later." She turned the lock on the doorknob and walked out in front of him. "Pull that shut, would you, please?"

"Sure."

Her cute little butt swished back and forth in her tight dress, giving him a nice view as they walked down the walkway toward his truck. He reached for the door latch to open it for her, and then helped her up into the cab with a hand on her butt.

She turned and gave him a raised eyebrow look.

"What?"

"Thanks for the boost up."

"You're welcome." He grinned thinking he liked how her soft butt cheek fit nicely in his palm. He had to adjust his cock behind his fly as he walked around the front of the truck to get in on the driver's side. It was going to be one uncomfortable night.

As they pulled out of the parking lot, he wondered about her. She apparently liked country music, which was a plus since it was his favorite too. Mexican food seemed to be something she enjoyed. What about steak, seafood, or Italian? Did she ride horses? Did she want kids? Was she a bed hog with the covers at night?

"What are you thinking about?" she asked as she turned toward him on the seat.

When he glanced her way, he could see her eyes sparkling in the dim light inside the cab. The color of her eyes fascinated him. He wasn't quite sure if they were blue or gray. They seemed to change with her moods, he noticed. "You. Why?"

"Me?"

"Yup."

"What about me?"

"I'm realizing I don't know that much about you even though you've been on the ranch for a couple of years. I know you are close to Peyton."

"Yeah. She and I are best friends, but I like all the girls on the ranch. I've become friends with all your brother's wives since they have hooked up with a Young brother."

"You seem to be protective of them, I noticed. At the bar the other night, you were ready to take on anyone and everyone who said anything bad about them."

"I would. They are like sisters to me."

"A little spitfire, I see."

She shrugged one shoulder as she glanced back out the front windshield. "Those girls have my back and I have theirs. I don't like people who talk with marbles in their mouths."

He laughed out loud. "I've never heard that saying before."

"No?" She smiled. "My dad used to say it all the time about people who talk about others when they don't know what they are talking about. You know how it sounds all garbled and stuff."

"Yeah, I get the picture."

"Don't your mom and dad have weird sayings like that?"

"I suppose. I never thought about it."

"I love your mom and dad. They are great people. They've raised some awesome kids."

"I'll pass it along."

She smacked him on the arm. "I'm not being facetious. I'm being truthful. All of you boys are thoughtful with others, kind, real gentlemen, and possibly the perfect cowboy."

"I don't believe that."

"I do. I've seen how your brothers are with their women. They love them without boundaries. They accept the little insecurities all women have and make them seem like the best thing in the world. You all are some of the best guys in the area, which is why so many women are after the two remaining Young brothers in the pool."

"I don't have women chasing me."

"Yes, you do. Haven't you seen the looks you get when you're at the diner or when you're interacting with guests? Those women would sell their soul to be with a real gentleman cowboy."

"Would you?" A slight smile played on her lips when he turned to glance her way.

"Yes, sir, I certainly would."

He shook his head as he grinned a little. He knew she was bold and outspoken most of the time. It was one of the things he liked about her. Actually, there were several things he liked about her, come to think of it. "I'll keep that in mind."

"I hope you do."

They pulled up to the restaurant on the outskirts of San Antonio. McGregor's Inn was known for their steaks. Juicy, thick, and cooked exactly how you wanted it had made their reputation for the best steakhouse in the state of Texas, which was an awesome feat in itself in the state where beef was prime. The inn looked like an old western bunkhouse. Two stories with huge barn doors that graced the front, opened to the wide dining area. There were stairs that led up to a large seating area at the top of the building where you could look down on the diners seated in the bottom. They prepared the steaks on an open grilling stand with mesquite wood, giving it a smoky flavor that would make your mouth water. They served baked potatoes with it, corn on the cob, salad, and hot rolls. Old tack, pictures, plows, and a huge fireplace decorated the area giving it that old farmhouse feel.

"Wow."

"You've never been here?"

"Nope. I love it. It's gorgeous in here," she said as they approached the hostess.

"Can I help you?"

"Yes, ma'am. We have reservations under the name Jonathan Young."

"Yes, sir. Your table will be ready in a moment. If you would like to take a seat, I'll tell the server you're here."

"Thank you." He placed his hand at the small of Mandy's back, guiding her to the seat near the door. The evening had turned brisk with a slight chill to the air. "Are you cold?"

"No. I'm good with my wrap."

"Okay." He'd done his best to make this a special night for them. It was the start of something wonderful, he hoped, so he'd dressed in his finest attire with his best black jeans, a sport coat, white long sleeved shirt open at the neck, and his finest black Stetson on his head.

Her gaze slipped over him from the top of his cowboy hat to the boots on his feet. "Did I tell you how nice you looked?"

"No."

"Well, you do. I love the dressed up cowboy look."

He studied her, his gaze sliding over her form. "I like your dress too. It's really nice on you."

"Thank you." She tilted her head to the side for a moment as she pursed her lips. "I think we look mighty good together."

"I do too."

"Mr. Young?"

Jonathan climbed to his feet. "Yes?"

"Right this way, sir. Your table is ready."

"Thank you." He splayed his hand at the small of her back again, to guide her along. He liked touching her way too much, but he couldn't help himself. Her lithe body fit well with his—in spite of her being a tiny little thing even in heels—in comparison to his six-foot-six frame.

He held out her chair as she whispered a soft thank you. The gesture wasn't something he did with any thought, it was the way he was raised. You take care of your woman by holding the door, holding her chair, walking on the busy side of the street to keep her safe, and you do everything you can to make her happy. Without much thought, he leaned down and kissed her shoulder. Her skin beneath his lips was soft and smelled like flowers. He liked her scent a whole lot.

Once he took his seat across from her, he found the view of her most enjoyable. Her cheeks were rosy and her eyes sparkled in the small flickering lamplight bouncing behind the globe on the table. Her lips looked kissable as he thought about how they felt under his when they'd made love the other night. Thinking about it as fucking, wasn't for him.

The waitress handed them their menus and as she opened hers to peruse the selections, he watched her over the top of his own. Having been to this particular restaurant many times, he already knew what he wanted, but it gave him a chance to study her. She didn't wear a lot of makeup, just a hint of color on her eyelids with a little mascara on her lashes, and a little swipe of tint to her lips. Her hair hung in long curls around her shoulders. The pink stripe from the top of her head to the ends of hair fascinated him. He often wondered why the bit of color.

She glanced over her menu and caught him staring. "What?"

"Nothing, why?"

"You're staring at me."

"I'm admiring the view."

Red crept up her neck, before fading across her face in a pretty pink color. She pressed a hand to her cheek. "You're embarrassing me."

"Why? You're a beautiful woman."

"No I'm not. I'm plain. There isn't anything special about me."

"Sure there is. You're a good friend, you are nice to people who come to the ranch as guests, and you make a special place for kids when they come. I've seen you around them."

She dropped her gaze to the tabletop as she set aside her menu. "I want to make them feel welcome, that's all."

"You do more than that. You are always playing with them, reading to them, and showing them a good time, all above and beyond your duties in the kitchen."

Her pretty bare shoulders lifted in a shrug. "It's nothing."

"Yes it is. You would be a great mom." She looked up at him and her face paled. "Did I say something wrong?"

"N-no."

"You look like you are about to be sick. Are you okay?"

Her throat visibly moved as she swallowed hard. "Yes. I'm fine."

"Did I say something wrong?"

"No. It's okay. I'm just a little warm."

"Do you need to go outside and get some air?"

She set aside her napkin and rose to her feet. "I'm going to run to the ladies room. I'll be right back."

She disappeared so fast, Jonathan thought she'd break a leg on those heels as she dashed through the throng of diners, heading for the bathroom.

What the hell did I say?

The waitress returned to get their drink orders, but he didn't know what Mandy might want. He'd order a bottle of wine, but he wasn't even sure she liked wine. "I'll wait until my date gets back."

"Very good, sir."

He tapped his fingers on the tabletop as he waited trying to figure out what he said that sent her to the bathroom in such a rush. When he looked around him, he noticed several other diners watching him as they sipped their wine, ate their food, or peeked over their menus. He considered going to the women's restroom to make sure she was okay, after she hadn't returned in several minutes. *She seemed rather pale. Maybe she is sick to her stomach or something.*

A moment later, he saw her come around the corner from where the restrooms were. "Are you all right?" he asked as he got up to pull out her chair.

"Yes. Sorry I took off like that."

"It's okay. I was worried about you though."

"Don't be. I'm fine. I, um, just got a little lightheaded is all."

"You aren't coming down with something are you?"

"I don't think so."

"You still look a little pale. Are you sure you don't want to go home?"

"No!" She sobered as she looked around and lowered her voice. "No. I don't want to ruin our evening. It's okay. I'm fine now."

He blew out a breath as the waitress approached their table. "Would you like some wine, Mandy? I would have ordered some, but I didn't know if you drank wine."

"Uh, sure, that's fine. Something red and sweet would be good."

He ordered a Merlot for them before he glanced her way again. "Are you sure you're all right?"

"I'm fine, Jonathan." She put her napkin in her lap. "Can we talk about something else?"

"Okay, like what?"

"What are your plans for the website for the ranch? I think you mentioned redoing the layout recently."

He took a minute to look at her closely before he decided to let the incident lie and began to explain what his plans were for the ranch. She would understand everything he said since her degree would be in graphic design, website management, and layout.

When the waitress returned a few moments later with their wine, she poured a small amount in his glass for him to taste and approve before giving Mandy hers. Mandy took a healthy gulp of the sweet liquid before setting her glass back down. For some reason, he got the impression the incident from earlier had her more rattled than she let on. Something bothered her so much, she'd got deathly pale and bolted for the bathroom, and by God he was determined to find out what it was so he could fix it for her if necessary.

* * * *

Mandy's stomach hurt from being in knots throughout dinner. Jonathan made a great dinner partner, but his personal questions made her uncomfortable. She shouldn't be though. He only wanted to get to know her, right?

After they'd finished their food, they had a dessert they shared over the candlelit table. He'd even fed her small bites of the chocolate cake from his spoon. Good grief, he was something special, and she really needed to let herself be with him and hope for the best.

As they drove down the interstate back toward Bandera, she watched him under the fan of her lashes. His hands were large with long tapered fingers, his arms were fit, and his chest was broad and well-muscled. His hair brushed against his collar with some of the curl showing beneath his cowboy hat. She liked it like that, but he probably thought he needed a haircut. His nose was straight and regal above his full lips. She knew he had a small dimple in his cheek when he smiled, which he did often when he was at home. She should know since she'd been watching him for so long.

When they had made love, he'd been a considerate lover, making sure her pleasure came before his own. Not many men did that these days.

He said he was shy, but she didn't see that in him even though he tended to be the quiet Young brother.

The cowboy thing was part of them like breathing. He couldn't get away from his upbringing no matter what he tried to do being the office hermit. He still rode horses, he still branded cattle when branding season came around, and he still liked the ranch life as a whole from what she could tell.

"Jonathan?"

"Yes?"

"I'm sorry for taking off earlier like that."

"It's okay. You obviously weren't feeling well or something."

"It wasn't that. I needed to take a minute is all."

"Was it something I said?"

"No." She looked out the windshield as she gathered her thoughts. How did you tell someone you were attracted to, that you were raped as a fifteen-year-old by someone close to you? She couldn't right now, maybe not ever. Her life had taken a bad turn back then and because of her upbringing, her parents wouldn't let her abort the child. She was glad she hadn't now because the family that had adopted her daughter had seemed very loving, and she figured they had given her little girl a good home. Someday, she hoped to be able to tell her daughter the real reason she hadn't kept her and raised her, but how do you explain to someone that she'd been conceived during a terrible act such as rape?

Mandy shivered as she rubbed her arms in an attempt to warm her soul. Even though it had been over ten years ago, she still vividly remembered the night it had happened. Her stepfather's brother had come to visit one Christmas. He hadn't visited often, but when he had before, he'd been her favorite uncle. He would spend time with her, listen to her talk about problems she was having as a teenager, and be the best friend she'd wished she had.

Christmas night, they had opened gifts. Hers from him had been a gorgeous butterfly necklace in solid silver with pretty multi-colored wings. When he'd placed it around her neck, she'd beamed. She loved it and loved him. "Thank you, Uncle Matt. It's perfect. I will wear it always."

"Fantastic. I'm glad you like it. Now give me a hug." He'd hugged her tight, pulling her onto his lap.

She hadn't thought anything about it at the time when he'd rubbed her back before bringing his hands around to her budding breasts, cupping them, and then pushing her back. "Shouldn't you be getting ready for bed? Santa will be coming soon."

"Oh come on, Uncle Matt. I don't believe in Santa."

He scolded her. "You should. He is going to be bringing you a wonderful present this year."

"Really?"

"Yes."

"All right then." She glanced at the clock on the wall, realizing it was getting late. "I'm going up to my room then. I will see you all in the morning."

"Good night," her parents had chimed in together.

"Sleep well, sweetie," Uncle Matt had said, giving her a wink before he took another sip of his drink.

She hadn't realized it at the time, but he'd been several sheets to the wind by the time she'd gone to bed.

Two hours later, she'd awoken to his hands on her hair. "Uncle Matt?" She rubbed her eyes.

"Sshh, sweetie. I just need to touch you."

"O-okay."

His hands had gone farther, brushing down her shoulders and across her breasts. "You are so pretty, filling out so nicely all over. Your breasts are very nice and your hips are perfect."

His hands had crept lower. "Please don't."

"It's okay, sweetheart. I won't hurt you," he said as he pulled her underwear down off her hips and legs.

But he had. He'd forced himself on her, telling her if she told anyone, they wouldn't believe her. She was nothing but a teenage girl and he was a man. Men could do what they wanted. Men were perfect.

She told her parents two weeks later when her period hadn't come.

They didn't believe her. They had assumed she'd been sleeping with someone in school and forced her to give the baby up.

It had been the worst ten months of her life. She'd been an outcast at school being a teenage mother, her grades had suffered, and her life had never been the same.

A tear slipped down her cheek, but she brushed it away before the man next to her could see.

She would never be taken advantage of again, not now, not ever.

Chapter Eight

Jonathan watched Mandy as she opened the door to her apartment. She'd been really quiet on the ride home, watching out the window without saying much of anything. Something was bothering her, and he wished she'd talk to him so he could help her.

She laid her wrap on the arm of the couch and turned to face him. Her eyes were sad.

"Tell me what's bothering you, Mandy. I want to help."

She smiled a pitiful smile as she touched his face. "I wish you could help me, Jonathan. No one can."

He pulled her into a tight hug, kissing her hair before resting his chin on her head.

She clung tightly to him, like she never wanted him to leave. "Make love to me."

"Are you sure you want that?"

"Yeah. I need you to help me erase some bad memories."

He pulled back to look into her eyes. The sadness in the depths broke his heart. If she wanted him to make love to her, then he would. He'd pour everything he had into making her smile again.

With both hands buried in her hair, he tipped her head to the side and brought his mouth down to hers. The sounds she made as he asked for permission to slip his tongue inside made him as hard as a damn rock. The soft whimpers and cute little sighs were almost too much for his libido to handle.

Her lips were soft enough to drown in as he pushed his tongue into her mouth to duel with hers. He loved kissing her. The feeling was something he hadn't been able to name, but he'd do his best to make sure she wasn't sorry she gave him her body.

Her hands fisted in his shirt, pulling him close enough that her breasts were crushed against him. The tips of her nipples poked him deliciously as she rubbed them all over his chest.

"Jonathan, please."

"Tell me what you want, Mandy."

"Love me."

He lifted her high into his arms as he headed down the hall to her bedroom. If she needed him to erase something from her mind, he'd do his best.

When he laid her on the bed, she sat up on her elbows to watch him undress. His jacket and shirt were disposed of before he quickly toed off his boots as her gaze moved over him. An appreciative smile curved her lips when he pushed his jeans down off his hips and over his legs.

"You are so nice to look at."

"Are you going to get undressed?"

"In a minute. I'm enjoying the scenery that is you, cowboy."

He moved to her side to take her lips. She wrapped her arms around his neck and pressed herself against him as he laid her back on the bed. He'd get to her clothes in a minute, right now he needed to taste her. He took her mouth in a soul-stopping kiss meant to take everything out of her mind but him. When he moved from her mouth to her cheek, and then her neck, she sighed as he nibbled at the flesh there. The shell of her ear would make a tasty morsel too, he decided.

Her legs started to move as she pressed her hips against his groin and shifted back and forth.

His cock ached with the need to be inside her. He wouldn't push the issue yet. There were things he wanted to do to her.

He lifted his mouth from her flesh. "Do you have any scarves?"

Her eyes were wide as she answered, "Yeah, in the drawer over there. Why?"

"Do you have anything wrong with your shoulders or arms?"

"No."

"Good." He got up and moved to her dresser to find what he searched for. When he returned to her side with several silky pieces of material in his hands, her eyes were wide with wonder.

"What are you going to do with those?"

"You'll see." His gaze moved over her body. "Sit up a minute." She followed instruction, and he reached for the zipper at the back of her dress. The bodice of her pink dress dipped forward revealing her perky, coral nipples. "Gorgeous." He ran his tongue along the edge of where her dress gapped. Her wispy sighs were his undoing.

He slipped a scarf over her wrist before tying it to the rungs of her headboard. After he secured the other, leaving her open to his mouth, he pulled the dress down over her hips, and then off her feet. "Oh hell." She'd gone commando. No underwear to be found and the lacy garter thing sent his thoughts spiraling out of control. "Those sexy heels and stockings are going to stay." He ran a finger around the edge of where they encircled her thigh and attached to the garter belt around her waist.

She shivered as she closed her eyes and arched her back.

A woman under his hands this responsive was a dream come true. He knew his tastes were a little out there, so finding this one was a treasure he would forever cherish.

He couldn't wait to get his cock buried in her sweet heat. For now, he would bring her up until she was ready to blow before he brought her back down.

The tips of her sexy breasts pulled into tight little nubs had his mouth watering. He couldn't help himself when he encircled one with the tip of his tongue.

She whimpered when he flicked it.

"I will leave your ankles unbound if you open for me and don't move."

Her breathes came out in small gasps as she spread her thighs. Her pussy glistened with juices. He wanted nothing more than to lick her clean and keep licking until she came in his mouth.

When he made room for his shoulders between her thighs, she sighed as she waited for him to do something. He smiled to himself knowing the anticipation was half the fun.

He blew a warm breath across her clit.

Her hips came up off the bed.

"Don't move." He'd leave the repercussions for her movement to her imagination.

Goose bumps broke out on her legs.

He licked the inside of her right thigh as he worked his way closer and closer to her pussy. She shivered when he ran his tongue up the crease between her thigh and her pussy lips.

One small swipe over her clit had more cream spilling from her.

"Such a sweet pussy."

When he glanced up from his position between her legs, he could see her straining against the bindings at her wrists as her chest rose and fell in a rapid pattern of need. Her heartbeat fluttered at her throat. Her mouth was open in a silent plea or a sigh, he wasn't sure which, but he could tell she was excited enough it wouldn't take much to throw her over the threshold into a mind-numbing orgasm.

He centered himself over her clit again, taking a few swipes of her juice on his tongue before he went to work bringing her to that orgasm she clung to by a thread.

She tossed her head back and forth on the pillow while she moaned louder with each pass of his tongue. "God, Jonathan, please, I need to come so badly."

A moment later, he pressed two fingers into her grasping cunt before he pushed his tongue against her clit and flicked it quickly. The second he pulled her clit into his mouth and bit down, she exploded into a screaming orgasm, his name a whisper on the wind.

Sweat clung to her body as he moved up over her abdomen, skimming his tongue along her flesh. She tasted sweet and salty at the same time. Her breasts quivered when he reached them, her nipples still pulled into hard points. A sigh escaped her lips when he brushed his tongue against the tip of one.

He moved between her parted thighs and pushed his cock into her heat. The feeling was something he'd never been able to put words to. All warm, wet, and silky and...*fuck.* He'd forgotten the condom.

Gritting his teeth, he pulled out, and rolled to his side. His cock and balls ached to be back inside her, but he had to protect them both. Children were something for the future, not right now.

"Jonathan?"

"Just a second. I have to get a condom before we continue this." The sensations running through his body had him strung tighter than a banjo string. If he didn't lose it the moment he got back inside her, it would be a miracle.

"Untie me."

He reached up and grabbed the end of the scarves to release her. She rolled to her other side, grabbed something out of the nightstand drawer, and then rolled back toward him. With a sexy little grin on her lips, she opened the package with her teeth before she slipped in over the head of his cock and then down the shaft.

"As hot as that was, I want to ride you, cowboy." In the next second, she was straddling his hips and taking his cock inside her in one push of her pussy. "Now that's perfect."

"Fuck yeah." White-hot need speared through him like a lightning bolt hitting the ground. His balls drew up against his groin, aching with pleasure almost to the point of pain.

"Dirty talker. I love it."

She lifted her hips before pushing them back down on his cock. Her pussy gripped him in a tight fist of warmth as she began to move. Her hands were braced on his chest while his gripped her hips, helping her move in just the right rhythm. His head felt like it was about to blow off when she increase her movements, bringing him to the edge of orgasm. He gritted his teeth trying to keep it from happening so soon. He wanted her to come for him too.

When she tipped her pelvis forward, dragging her clit over his pelvis, he knew she was close. The small whimpers and increasing sighs told him as much.

"Come for me, darlin'."

"Oh God."

The excited sigh from her lips as he felt the warm liquid dribble from her pussy brought on his own orgasm as he shouted his pleasure to the ceiling.

She draped herself over his chest, tucking her head beneath his chin as she wrapped herself around him.

"Mmm. That was perfect."

"I agree," he said, running his hands down her back. He loved the feeling of her skin beneath his hands. The softness reminded him that she was all woman and one he could totally see himself with for the long haul. Did that mean he wanted something more permanent with her? He wasn't so sure, but he definitely wanted to see how far this thing would go, if she would be willing.

They lay like that for several minutes while he listened to her soft breathing and felt her heart slow in the aftermath of their explosive lovemaking.

"Will you stay?" she asked quietly.

"If you want me to."

"I would love to wake up with you next to me. I'll make breakfast."

"Now, how could I possibly refuse that offer?"

She giggled a little as she moved to the side of his body and rolled off the bed. After she shoved her hair out of her face, she slipped off her heels so she was walking around in her sexy stockings. The sight of her naked ass did wonderful things to him.

He propped himself up on his elbow as he watched her putter around her room, grabbing his clothes and laying them across the chair in the corner before she grabbed his dress shirt and put it on.

"How come you get clothes and I'm laying here buck naked?"

"Because I like you buck naked."

"Listen, baby girl. We need to have a discussion on who is in charge here."

"Oh?"

"Yes, ma'am."

When she turned to look at him, her eyes sparkled with a bit of a challenge. *So that's how it's gonna be, huh?* He crooked his finger in her direction.

She only raised an eyebrow as she placed her hands on her hips.

A brat. He loved a dare.

Before she could react, he vaulted off the bed, catching her around the waist.

She screamed as he tossed her over his shoulder.

A tiny fist hit him mid-back.

In retaliation, he brought his hand down on her ass cheek, swift and hard.

"Ouch! You didn't just spank me?"

"That was a warning."

"Or what?"

He took a seat on the bed and brought her over his knees with a hand on her back, her head down toward the floor and her ass high in the air. He yanked the shirt up, baring her ass before one hand came down swiftly on her right butt cheek, leaving a nice red handprint.

"Son of a bitch!"

"I warned you."

"What the hell?"

His hand came down again in three rapid swats to her left butt cheek.

She wiggled to get free, but he put a hand on the spot he knew stung from his spanking.

"Lie still and take your punishment for being a brat."

After a momentary hiss, she quit moving as he delivered another six quick slaps to her behind, alternating between the right and the left. When he was finished, he pulled her back up, bringing her up to his lap.

Her makeup had run where she'd silently wept from the stinging spanking, so he wiped it from her cheeks. Somehow, he'd been given the impression she probably needed the release tears would bring. Maybe it was the sadness in her eyes that had drawn him to spank her or the challenge in her stance, but whatever it was, he'd been pulled into spanking her for her own good.

"Why did you spank me?"

"I won't tolerate disrespect."

"I'm sorry," she whispered, even though her eyes were clearer and brighter now.

If she reacted this way to punishment, she might fit very nicely into his life. "You're forgiven. It's over now. We won't talk about it again."

"Jonathan?"

"Yes?"

"I like when you tied me up."

"I liked it too."

"Can we do that again?"

He smiled. Things were looking up if she was open to experimenting with his little fetishes. He could really get into doing more with her in the future.

"Yes, darlin', we can."

* * * *

The next day as Mandy worked on preparing the food for lunch at the ranch, she winced as her butt stung from the spanking she'd received from Jonathan the night before. It was strange to think about the weight that had been lifted from her shoulders after she'd cried. She'd felt lighter and freer than she had in years.

After she'd fixed him breakfast, he'd kissed her softly, grabbed his hat, and left for home. Something had changed with their relationship in those moments they'd bonded over her stinging ass cheeks. He'd become the man she needed in her life, the one who would understand her, forgive her, and would hopefully love her until they were both old and gray.

God, she sounded like such a sap, but her happy heart wouldn't be quiet today.

Peyton came through the double doors of the kitchen and grabbed a lemon bar from the cooling rack. "You look gorgeous today. What did you do different?"

"Nothing. Why?"

"Your cheeks are a pretty pink and your eyes are sparkling." Peyton tipped her head to the side and grinned. "You look like a girl in love."

Mandy put her hand over Peyton's mouth and shushed her. "Be quiet. Don't be saying that too loudly. Nina will be planning a wedding before the weekend if she hears you."

Peyton moved her hand and whispered, "You are in love. I knew it!" She took another bite of her lemon bar. "Nice night with Jonathan?"

A heated blush crept up her face as she went back to slicing tomato. "Yeah. It was pretty special."

"I can tell. I think I heard him sneaking in this morning."

She glanced over her shoulder at Peyton and said, "Keep it close to your chest, please. I don't need gossip running rampant through the guest ranch."

"Sure, honey. I won't say a word."

The gleam in Peyton's eyes didn't bode well for Mandy, she knew. Her friend had a tendency of sticking her nose in where it didn't belong sometimes. "Are we having a girl's night out again soon?"

"I don't know. Have you talked to the others?"

"No, but I think we should. At least once a month is a good idea to get everyone away from the house and their kids."

"I'm sure the others would enjoy it. They had fun the last time."

"Oh, Candace told me she was putting together a bachelor auction for the children's hospital she helps raise money for. You know the one that Samantha did the benefit concert for?"

"Yeah. That sounds like fun."

"I thought so too, although I wouldn't be able to buy anyone. We could still get really drunk and set you up with some hunky cowboy. Jonathan wouldn't have to know."

"I couldn't do that to him."

"Maybe Candace can get him to go up there."

"Jonathan? Yeah, right. He's way too shy."

"I bet he would do it for her. They are like this." She crossed her fingers and held them up.

"I know."

"Does that bother you?"

"A little, but I know they are just friends. Candace is his sister-in-law. He would never do anything to hurt Joshua."

"Besides, he's all tied up in you."

Tied up. Now there's a thought. I wonder if he would let me tie him to the bed like he did me? "I should talk to Candace about this auction. If Jonathan got up there, I could bid on him and have him at my mercy for however long I want."

"Now you're talkin'!"

Mandy grinned, thinking of the possibilities. They were endless.

She arranged the tomatoes on a plate to put in the service area so those who wanted them could take them or not before she got the salad mix out and put some in the large bowl. Tongs went in next for serving along with bottles of dressing and thick slices of French bread. For lunch today, lasagna.

Soon, it was time to put lunch out for the guests. Mandy and the other kitchen workers got the food out on the hot table as Peyton went to ring the bell, letting the guests know it was time to eat.

There were a few families staying on the ranch right now with several small children. The weather was still warm for October in Texas, which meant most of them spent the day in the pool area, riding, hiking, or hanging out with the animals.

Mandy smiled as she watched everyone file in for lunch. The family always sat at two large tables at the front of the room and the guests had several picnic type tables to choose from. The family always waited until the guests were served before they got their own plates, which always made Mandy proud to know them. The guests came first in everything at Thunder Ridge.

She turned to see Jonathan come around the corner of the stairs. His office sat back behind them in the corner near where his parents had their private quarters. She'd been in his office a time or two and knew he kept it quite tidy. Everything in its place. His desk was a large oak monstrosity that took up most of the space. It suited him though since he was such a big guy.

His gaze fixed on her the moment he realized she was there. The stare burned with something she wasn't sure she wanted to put a name to. His brown eyes took in everything about her from the top of her head down, stopping to focus on her breasts for a moment before a crooked little grin creased his face, showing the dimple in his cheek.

Mandy had to shift her stance in a vain attempt to relieve the pressure that look caused between her thighs. The man could send her into a combustible state with nothing more than a glance. Damn him.

Jonathan took a seat at the table as they waited for the guests to be served, but he never once stopped his ogling of her. The heat from his scrutiny seared her skin, burning her clear through. She blew her hair off her forehead in an attempt to cool herself off.

His smile widened.

He knew what he did to her, the rat bastard.

She cleared her throat as she pulled her attention back to the guest in front of her ready to serve up some lasagna, garlic bread, and green beans. "There is salad to your left, sir."

"Thank you."

"You're welcome."

The man's attention focused on her breasts where they pressed against her tank top. "Is there something else I can help you with?"

"That depends."

"On?"

"What time do you get off work?"

"Seven."

"Would you like to have a drink with me?"

She glanced at the growing line behind him before focusing back on his leering face. Something about him reminded her of the man who raped her. She shuddered before she pulled back her shoulders and said, "No, sir."

The man frowned as his disgusting look ricocheted back to her face. "Aren't you supposed to make the guests happy?"

"What I do on my own time is my own business."

"Problem?" Jonathan appeared at her elbow.

"Yeah. I thought the employees were supposed to take care of the guests."

"They are, sir."

"Well then tell blondie here she needs to go out with me tonight."

"No, sir. I will not."

"What?"

"Mandy is an employee here, yes, but she's also her own person. If she doesn't want to go out with you, she is more than capable of making that decision herself. We do not force our employees to do anything."

"That's fucking bullshit!"

"What's your name, sir?"

"Leon Ornado."

"Mr. Ornado. Your bill will be credited for the days remaining on your stay. You will leave the ranch now. Pack your belongings and be gone within the hour."

"I'm not leaving."

"Yes you are."

"Who the hell are you to tell me to leave?"

In the next moment the entire clan of Young men stood around him. "I am one of the owners of this piece of property, and my family will back my decision to insist that you leave…now."

"Fuck you! Fuck you all!" The man threw down his plate on the serving bar, turned on his heels, and disappeared out the main lodge doors.

"I'll make sure he's gone," Jeff said, as he nodded to his family before following the man outside.

Mandy's whole body quivered with the adrenaline pumping through her. The family stood beside her as Jonathan took her in his arms, running soothing strokes down her back.

"Ssh. It's okay. He's gone."

"Thank you."

"You are part of this family, Mandy. We stand beside those who are ours."

She held on tight for a moment before stepping back. "I need to finish serving lunch."

"Go into the kitchen and take a minute to gather yourself. I'll handle serving for now."

"You'd do that?"

"Of course. I wield a mean spoon." Jonathan grinned as he shooed her through the double doors and took up his place behind the hot table.

She paused for a moment in the doorway as she watched him charm the pants off the guests with his quick wit, charming smile, and cowboy way.

God, she loved him.

Chapter Nine

Mandy made her way across the darkened ground toward the big barn in the distance. After supper, she'd asked where he'd gotten off to since he'd disappeared right after he'd eaten. "Jonathan?"

"In the tack room."

She smiled as she made her way down the well-lit center aisle of the huge structure. The barn was two story and big enough to house most of their horses in individual stalls should they find the need like during a storm or something. It also housed a huge indoor arena for working the horses if they wanted to do so in an enclosed area. Joey took care of the horses on the place, but each of the boys had their own mount.

As she came around the corner, she found him sitting in a chair at the desk with a bridle in his hands working soap into the leather. "Whatcha doin'?"

He looked up, smiled, and then let his gaze roam down her frame. "Cleaning some tack."

"I thought that was Joey's job."

"We all help out on occasion, besides it's kind of soothing to do. You can do a lot of thinking while you are working the soap into the piece." He leaned toward her and pushed out another chair. "Have a seat."

She took the chair, turned it around, and straddled it. His eyebrow rose over his left eye as his grin widened.

"Done in the kitchen for the day?"

"Yep."

"What brings you out here?"

"You. I had to ask where you disappeared to after supper."

He shrugged as he went back to his work. "I figured you'd be busy for a bit and this stuff is filthy."

She saw the dirt-caked towel across his knee as well as the one in his hands. "Wow. Yeah, it really is."

"It can rub the animal raw if it doesn't get cleaned regularly."

"Where's Joey?"

"Off running around town somewhere, I guess. He's been hanging out a lot with one of the neighbor girls. I think he's going to get himself into trouble with her, but he won't listen. I hope he finds a nice girl to settle down with soon."

"Doesn't he ride rodeo?"

"Yeah, sometimes. Bronc mostly."

"Cool."

"Why all of the interest in Joey suddenly?"

"I'm not *interested* if that's what you mean. I already have one Young brother to keep up with. Two would be too much."

"Remember that."

"Jealous?"

"Yep, even if he is my brother. I like having you under me."

"Or on top of you."

"That too."

He set the bridle aside on the desk before he turned back toward her and crooked his finger. She rose to her feet, sauntering closer as she wondered what he had in mind. There were a lot of things he could use to make this a very enjoyable encounter, right there under his hands. Saddles, bridles, leather straps, blankets, latigo, and more, were at his disposal.

When she got close enough, his fingers began to work the buttons on the front of her blouse as she worked herself between his parted thighs. As each inch of skin was exposed, he followed the path with his mouth, licking and sucking bits of flesh until she tingled all over. She buried her hands in his thick hair, knocking his hat to the floor behind the chair.

The scent of leather was one of her favorites, making her hot and needy from the moment she'd stepped into the room surrounding herself with all the tack.

The second her blouse was completely open, he pulled it from the waistband of her jeans before pushing it off her shoulders, leaving her in nothing but a soft pink bra with lacy edges

With a grasp on the straps at her shoulders, he pulled each one down over her arms until her bra gapped at the front. He slowly peeled the material down until her breasts were free to be devoured by his mouth.

She moaned the moment he took the right nipple between his lips. "We should probably shut the door."

He shook his head, but didn't lose his suction on her breasts.

"What if we get caught?"

He tongued the tip for a moment before he finally released her and looked up. "What if we do?"

Her body flushed as she thought about someone walking in on them having sex in the tack room surrounded by the tangy scent of leather.

"The thought excites you, doesn't it."

It wasn't a question. It was a statement and one she couldn't deny. She'd never had the chance to be anything close to an exhibitionist, but the thought of people watching them fuck made her hotter than a comet.

He watched her face as he unbutton her jeans, grasped them along with her panties at the waist and slowly peeled them down her body. Standing in front of him naked except for the jeans around her ankles, with the cool night air caressing her back from the open door, had cream dribbling from her pussy.

"I can smell your arousal."

Her breath hitched.

One finger spread her juices from her clit to her ass before he nudged the tip of his finger inside her.

"Oh God."

"Like that do you?"

Her answer came out as a soft moan as she tipped her head back on her shoulders and shivered.

"You are so beautiful."

He removed his hand from between her legs, much to her dismay, but when he grabbed a fistful of her hair, forced her to straddle his thigh, and then took her mouth in a soul-shattering kiss, she couldn't help but lose herself to his touch. His mouth and tongue took possession of her in a way she'd never imagined would turn her on. It did.

The friction of his jean-clad thigh along her clit had her hurting with the need to come. She rubbed herself along his thigh, bringing herself to the peak of pleasure until his hand came down in a hard slap to her butt cheek.

"No cheating."

"Please, Jonathan."

"Nope. You'll come when I say you can." He pushed her back, forcing her to stand on shaking legs as he came to his feet in front of her. "Remove your boots and jeans." He watched her through dark intense eyes as she finished stripping off her clothing. "There is a saddle there on that stand. I want your ass on the seat sideways, legs spread."

Excitement sizzled along her nerves as she moved toward where the saddle stood. She didn't know what he had planned, but God, help her, she wanted everything he had to give. When she put her butt on the hard, cold seat, she hissed at the sensations the friction caused on her heated skin.

He pushed a long, wood toolbox closer to her, indicating she should brace her feet on the edges as he sat down between her spread thighs.

"Gorgeous," he whispered reverently as he spread her labia with his fingers and blew a soft puff of air over her wet pussy.

The moment his tongue flicked against her clit, she almost lost control of her orgasm.

"Don't come until I tell you."

"I'm going to die."

"No you won't. Be the good girl I know you can be."

For him, she would. She would do anything he wanted her to do as long as he continued to torture her poor flesh with his mouth and tongue.

She whimpered softly as he pressed his nose into the crease between her pussy and her thigh, ran his tongue up the crack, and then hummed his appreciation over her clit.

Her hands fisted in his hair, trying desperately to push his head against her to give her more and more of the tormenting pleasure.

As he began to rapidly flick her clit with his tongue, she could feel her orgasm creeping up her legs in a warm rush that would soon burst through her pelvis.

Then he did the most torturous thing he could do, he started to slowly lick her clit in soft, small strokes. He gripped her butt in his hands and held her to his mouth, making little humming noises as he feasted on her flesh.

The minute he sucked her clit into his mouth and bit down, she couldn't stop the rush of climax that broke over her in a tingling wave meant to leave her mindless. She came apart with his name on her lips in a high cry of satisfaction that bounced off the rafters over their heads.

He continued to lick softly as she came down from her high and her heart rate slowed to a slow gallop. "I'm sorry."

He lifted his head, her juices still clinging to his lips as he swiped his tongue over the surface of his mouth. "You came without permission."

"I know. I need to be punished." She flushed hot just thinking about his hand on her ass, swiftly smacking until it burned.

"I think you like that too much."

"But..."

He smiled and leaned down to kiss her with long, slow movements of his mouth on her lips. His hands began a smooth journey over her breasts, bringing the nipples back to achy points. When he pinched the tip between his thumb and first finger, she almost came off her perch. The sensation was incredibly painful, but pleasurable at the same time.

Unable to contain herself any longer, she grasped at his belt buckle in wild desperation to part the metal from the leather. "Son of a bitch. I can't get it loose."

"Easy, little filly." He unbuckled it himself, before parting his jeans to free his cock from the confines.

She worked her hand into his jeans to grasp his cock in her shaking hands. "I need this. I need you."

"In a minute. No rush."

"Yes there is. I'm so fucking horny, my head feels like it is about to explode."

"You just had an orgasm. Are you telling me it wasn't enough?"

She grabbed his face between her hands and brought his mouth close to hers. "That was the tip of the iceberg. I hurt from wanting you. You've been driving me crazy all day with sexy looks, little winks, and those dimpled smiles of yours. Every time I looked your way, I could feel my pussy getting hot and throbbing. Don't torture me anymore, please." She pushed his jeans down past his hips before she grabbed his cock in her palm again. "I want this."

He didn't even bother to take his pants all the way off before he grabbed a condom from his back pocket, slipped it on, and eased himself into her.

Her cunt quivered around him as he pushed inside. Her heart hammered against her ribs as he began a slow, hip-grinding thrust.

"When we're done fucking like this, I aim to take your ass."

Holy mother of God.

"For now, I'm going to fuck you slow and easy until you are squirming on my cock."

Heat flushed her skin a bright red as he did what he said, slow and easy. It didn't take long for her to realize what a sadist he was, but what did that make her? She never thought of herself as a masochist. However, the pain he'd dished out with his hand on her ass left an enjoyable impression. The notion might be something they would need to explore further. For now, she needed to focus on the feel of him deep inside her. The hardness spreading her wide, made her want to whimper and moan while he eased in and then out.

She leaned back on her hands as she gripped the pommel of the saddle in one hand and the cantle in the other. Her toes cramped from where she had her feet up on the edges of the toolbox he'd been sitting on when he'd ate her like a starving man. In this position, she could see his cock penetrating her with the slow rocking of his hips. The sight brought more wetness between her legs. "Good God, that's hot."

"You like watching me fuck you?"

"Yes. I've never seen anything so sexy in my life."

"Do you want to come again before I take you from behind?"

"I've never had a man there so I'm not sure how to answer that question."

He kept talking as he continued to push his cock into her pussy. "I love the thought of being your first anal experience."

"You won't hurt me?"

His movements stopped as he looked down into her eyes. "God no. I would never hurt you. You can stop things any time you want. I want it to be a pleasurable experience for you too." She moaned when he pulled his cock from her center. "Roll over on the saddle with your butt in the air, your feet on the toolbox and spread your cheeks for me."

She shivered as she followed his instructions, not sure what the sounds were he was making behind her as he opened and closed a couple of drawers on the desk. When she felt a dollop of cold liquid hit her hot ass, she hissed between her teeth.

Anticipation crawled over her skin in a wave of desire she couldn't control. Fear made her breathing coming out fast and hard. She'd heard anal sex hurt, but she trusted Jonathan with her heart and soul, knowing he would never intentionally hurt her.

As she reached back to spread herself for him, she felt the hard head of his cock at her back hole.

"I'm going to go very slow. I want you to tell me everything you are feeling whether it be pleasure or pain. All right?"

"Okay," she whispered as he eased himself in.

The first sensation she experienced was a burn, a sweet burn. "It burns a little."

He stopped moving. "Are you okay?"

"Yes. It's a good feeling. I like the little bite of pain."

He pushed a slight bit forward again.

"Oh, oh, oh."

"Talk to me, Mandy."

"It's good. Holy hell, it's good. The pressure makes me feel full in a good way." She felt her pussy cream. "God, that's hot."

He continued to push forward inch by inch until she felt the hair on his pelvis brush against her ass. "I'm all the way in. Tell me what you're feeling."

"Oh my God. It's fantastic. I don't know how to describe it." She shivered. "What now?"

"I'm going to start to move. I'll go slow."

As he started pulling his cock out before shoving it back in, she thought her head would explode from the emotions screaming through her body. She felt hot and needy, desperate to come in a climax that would surpass anything she'd felt in the past. "I need to come, Jonathan. God, please, let me come."

His pace picked up in quick, hard thrusts, shoving her hard against the saddle under her. His breathing echoed in the small room. She could hear him grinding his teeth together in a vain attempt to hold back his own orgasm.

"I need, oh God, I need to come."

"Come for me, Mandy."

Lights exploded behind her eyelids as her whole body shivered in response to his command. Her pussy throbbed and spilled cum on the floor beneath them as she lost all coherent thought for the entire time it took her body to absorb the climax she'd just had.

She slumped over the saddle beneath her, exhausted from their sexcapades, as he eased himself from her ass and disposed of the condom.

"You okay?"

"I'm better than okay. I can't move."

"Do I need to help you?"

"You mean you can think coherently right now because I certainly can't." He laid a sharp slap on her naked butt, bringing her up straight. "That wasn't very nice."

"I thought it was. You have a very nice ass. I enjoyed fucking it tremendously."

She couldn't help the smile that spread across her face at his offhanded compliment. "Thank you for easing me into that."

He reached out, touching her cheek with his palm. "Baby, I would do anything for you. I hope you know that."

Her happy heart sang with delight as his words filled the emptiness in her soul. This thing between them might just work out. *God, I hope so, otherwise he could really hurt me.*

* * * *

Jonathan shook his head as he tried to focus on the screen in front of him so he could get some work done. It had become harder and harder to get anything accomplished in his office since he kept thinking about Mandy and how things had went from casual to serious in such a short time. If he wasn't careful, he would find himself ass deep in love with her.

Sorry buddy, but I think you're there already.

"Aw, hell."

He pushed back his chair, tossed his pen on the desk, and jumped to his feet. He needed some air and fast.

Quick steps took him through the main lodge and out the side door as he headed for the barn. Riding always helped to clear his mind when he was a kid, maybe it would do the trick this time. Sure couldn't hurt, he figured.

As he reached the cooler interior of the barn and let his eyes adjust to the darkness, he caught a glimpse of Joey working with one of the new horses in the arena. He didn't want to answer any questions from his nosey brothers, so he quietly retrieved his horse from the paddock to the right, tied him to the post in the barn, and got his tack from the tack room.

A light shown through the office doorway as he passed. He looked inside and saw Jeff sitting at the desk doing some work. "I'm going riding. I need to think."

"You okay?" Jeff asked, looking up from his paperwork. "Need to talk?"

"Yeah, I'm okay. I'm headed to the pond. I'll be back in a bit."

"Okay."

The moment he had everything in place, he unhooked his gelding and walked him out the back, which led to the corral. The back entrance where they brought the guests in and out from their rides stood empty. No one was around except the horses waiting tied to their spots, happily munching on hay.

He gathered the reins in his left hand, stuck his foot in the stirrup and hoisted himself up into the saddle. His horse sidestepped a moment, anxious for a run. The appaloosa was one of the different animals on the ranch. Most of the horses they had were quarter horses because of their stamina on the ride, but he'd always preferred the eager to please attitude and great disposition of this breed.

A light tap of his heels to the animal's side, and the horse took off like a shot.

He ate up the ground under his pounding hooves like his ass was on fire. Maybe it was.

Wind whipped by him as the junipers became a blur. He leaned over the horse's neck, urging him on to more speed. They flew over the rocky ground, headed for where, he wasn't sure. He needed this solitude, this quiet moment to gather his thoughts.

The mud pit the family enjoyed going mudding in didn't stop him, although good memories assaulted him with the glance at the terrain.

A small tree branch smacked him in the leg as he sped down the trail.

He could see the neighbor's houses from the top of the hill where he finally stopped to rest his winded horse. The animal's side billowed in and out while he tried to catch his breath. "Sorry, boy." The horse tossed his head for a moment as he pawed at the ground. Jonathan smiled. His horse still wanted to run, but Jonathan knew he needed to give him a little break. "Easy, boy. We will go slower."

Jonathan tapped him with his heels while keeping a tight grip on the reins so the horse knew he wanted him to walk for a bit.

The air seemed crisper today. October could go either way in Hill Country. This year, fall seemed to have a colder tinge to the air.

The horse picked his way along the path, avoiding tree branches, huge rocks, and areas where the footing might not be so safe. This animal was well trained for trail riding.

Quiet surrounded him. Not even the sound of an insect broke the solitude he'd craved when his butt hit the saddle this morning.

The reins were gripped loosely in his left hand, not that he really needed to guide the appaloosa. The saddle creaked under him, soothing his soul like nothing else could. The trees, the bushes, the silence, the animal beneath him, and the sun on his shoulders would do more for his spirit than anything, which seemed funny because he normally worked in the office from sunup until sundown on the websites and marketing.

I guess I really am a cowboy at heart.

Jonathan headed to the pond. It had always been one of his favorite spots on the ranch and today, he wanted to sit and think.

As the horse approached the area, he saw a deer standing at the edge of the water, silently sipping the cool, clear liquid until its thirst had been sated. The animals in the area used this lot for watering, so it wasn't unusual to see wildlife here. He pulled his horse to a stop as he waited for the skittish deer to finish. When the doe lifted her head, she spotted him across the water, turned to the left and spirited off at a quick run.

The moment the deer disappeared through the brush, his horse walked to the edge of the pond and put his head down to drink. Jonathan dismounted and ground tied the animal knowing he wouldn't wander too far.

His boots crunched the rock beneath his feet as he moved toward the big rocks at the top of the pond where the water trickled down from the stream above. It was the perfect perch to watch the area and to think.

He sat down on the biggest rock, hooking one boot on a smaller rock below him and one on a rock to his left. He glanced up at the blue skies over his head, realizing it was very close to the color of Mandy's eyes, that pure sky blue.

Images of their relationship over the last few weeks sped across his mind. Things had been going good. They were communicating, enjoying each other on an intimate level and it was something he hadn't experienced with anyone else. It was kind of nice. Their time together had been special. She'd definitely had a good time when they had made love. Talks between them were open, honest, and great, but he still felt she was holding something back. What though? Surely there wasn't anything in her past that would be an issue. He didn't care if she'd been into drugs and stuff during her teenage years. Hell, they had all experimented at one time or another.

Nothing during their times making love seemed out of sorts. She'd enjoyed being tied up from what she'd said. Anal sex hadn't bothered her even though she'd never experienced it before.

"Am I really falling in love with her?" he asked the nothingness around him looking for the answer without having to delve too far into his soul.

His heart whispered back an affirmative yes.

He couldn't really picture his life without her in it. She'd been such a part of Thunder Ridge for the last few years that she'd seemed part of the family even though she hadn't been dating any of his brothers. He couldn't picture her with any of them though. He knew her body and he knew she'd become something special to him, even if he'd only been seeing her for a few weeks. Their bond had grown to the point where he wanted her in his life on a permanent basis. Did that mean marriage? Maybe. Right now, he needed to see where her heart was in the scheme of things. If she couldn't see herself with him for the long haul, he wasn't sure what he'd do. It would be difficult for him to be around her all the time and not want her.

The crunch of hooves alerted him to someone approaching. He knew his brothers came here often too, so it didn't surprise him when Jeff rode into the clearing. *Right on time.*

"Hey. I thought I'd join you. You sounded like you might need someone to talk to."

"Yeah, maybe."

"So. What's up?"

"My relationship with Mandy."

Jeff dismounted and ground tied his horse near Jonathan's appaloosa. "Do you want to talk about it?"

Jonathan sighed. He was close to all of his brothers, but Jeff was the eldest and held a bit of big brother attitude on his shoulders. He wanted to be able to fix everyone's problems all the time. His efforts didn't usually work out very well, but it might not hurt to get his opinion.

"I think I'm falling in love with her."

"What makes you think so?"

"Well, I can't seem to get her off my mind. Sex has been great between us and she really seems to be into me too."

"True. She's been chasing you for three years now."

"I know and we are getting along great."

"Why do you think you're in love with her though? What makes her any more special than anyone else you've dated?"

"She gets me. We understand each other. We have a lot in common, and she's open to my particular brand of sexual tendencies."

"So she would make a good pet?"

"If you mean pet as in submissive, maybe, but if you mean pet like in dog, no. She's independent, not a doormat."

"I didn't realize you were looking for a dominant/submissive type relationship."

"I didn't either until she came along. I mean, I'm not twenty-four seven BDSM, but I do like a little spice to my sex life and she was open to experimenting so I guess that's good."

"Yeah, it's better than finding out she's grossed out by it."

Jonathan glanced sideways at his brother. Jeff had grown older in the last few years, but he seemed very happy in his relationship with his live-in girlfriend and their children. A wedding was being planned for next June and it made Jonathan happy to see his brother finally come to his senses. It was about time. "How's the wedding planning coming?"

"It's been hell." Jeff sighed as he shifted on the rock he'd taken a seat on.

"Why?"

"Terri is driving me nuts with all the details and it's still several months off. I'll be glad when it's over."

"You're happy though?"

Jeff smiled as he tipped his hat back on his head with a finger to the brim. "Yeah. I can't believe I didn't marry her before. I don't know what I was thinking."

"You were thinking about how your ex hurt you and you were afraid Terri would too."

"Maybe, but she's proven to me that she's here to stay, so I'll be happy to put a ring on her finger."

"I'm glad you two are together. She's good for you. She doesn't put up with your shit."

Jeff punched him in the shoulder. "And you do?"

"Hell no. I've got your number, big brother."

"You and Joey are the only two unattached Young brothers left. Are you getting lots of attention because of it? I know the local women are becoming a lot bolder in their pursuit."

"I don't really see it. Maybe Joey is, but I don't get that kind of attention. Not that I'm aware of anyway."

"I see the way they look at you two when you are around the bar with us. You aren't paying much attention because you are kind of shy."

"Yeah, I guess, but I'm really thinking it's time to find that special lady."

"Well, then you need to settle down with someone and take yourself off the market. Leave the pursuing to Joey. He's up for the challenge."

They laughed in unison knowing their youngest sibling could totally handle more than one woman pursuing him.

"So what are you going to do about Mandy?"

"I'm not sure. I came out here because I'm confused about my feelings for her. I like her a lot and I think we are good together, but something is telling me she's not being completely honest with me."

"Have you talked to Peyton? Maybe she could give you some insight."

"No. That might be a good idea. Mandy and Peyton have been friends for quite a long time. She might be able to tell me what's going on in Mandy's head."

"I suggest you talk to her then."

"Okay. I will. Tonight. After supper."

They both stood and walked back to where their horses had stopped to munch on some grass. After they had both mounted, they turned toward home, riding in silence, lost in their own thoughts, until the main lodge came into view.

Jonathan loved the old house with its wraparound porches and antique pieces on the front area next to the rocking chairs. He loved to go out there with his coffee in the mornings and just think. It was peaceful.

"What the hell?"

"What?"

Jeff jerked his head to the side, indicating the front of the main lodge. "Look."

Chapter Ten

Terri stood in front of the porch in a long white gown, holding a bouquet of flowers. Her family and his stood beside her as she stepped forward to meet them.

Jonathan grinned. He'd been in on the surprise for his eldest brother. Thank God Jeff had taken the bait and come after him when he'd stopped at the office to tell him where he would be. His eldest brother couldn't stay out of other people's business if his life depended on it, so Jonathan knew if he told him he needed to think, his brother would follow.

"What's going on, Terri?" he asked as he dismounted from his horse.

"I know I've been driving you nuts with wedding planning, and I know we were going to wait until next year, but I decided I didn't want to wait anymore. I've waited on your ass long enough, Jeff Young. Will you marry me right here, right now in front of your family and mine?"

Jeff glanced around him as a slow smile lifted the corners of his mouth. "You bet!" He swept her off her feet and carried her to where the preacher stood waiting at the end of the walkway. When he set her on her feet and turned expectantly toward the preacher, every one of his family laughed. "Sorry I'm not in my finery."

"You look like the cowboy I fell in love with."

The families took their places standing behind the couple as the preacher went through the wedding ceremony.

Jeff frowned as he turned toward his family. "I don't have a ring. I haven't had a chance to go shopping."

Nina stepped forward holding out her first wedding set in her hands. "I would be honored if you would wear mine, Terri.

Jeff is my eldest, and as such, is entitled to the first wedding set James ever bought for me."

"Thank you, Mom." Terri kissed her on the cheek as Jeff took the rings in his hand.

"I love you, Mom," Jeff said, as he turned back toward Terri and repeated the vows as he slipped the beautiful rings onto her finger. "You're mine now, woman. No running off on me. You're stuck."

"Like glue, baby, like glue." Terri reached up, wrapped her hand behind Jeff's head, and crushed their mouths together while the rest of the family cheered.

Jonathan looked across the group, and his gaze caught on Mandy. There were tears swimming in her eyes as she watched Terri and Jeff greet everyone in the group. She fit, that's all there was to it. She had become part of this family over the last few years, and he couldn't see her not being here for things like this, Christmases, birthdays, anniversaries, births, and everything else families did.

When she looked his way, he smiled when she automatically started toward him. Surely it was a sign, something that told him they belong together.

"Hey," she said, stopping in front of him.

She looked gorgeous in her pink off the shoulder dress and pink toenails. She wasn't wearing any shoes. The smile on her lips made her eyes sparkle. Happiness radiated from her. Maybe she was ready for them to become more.

"Hey," he replied, reaching out to touch the curl lying on her shoulder. "You look beautiful."

"Thanks. You look pretty handsome yourself."

He glanced down, taking in his dirty jeans, button down western shirt, and dusty boots before he looked back up into her eyes. "Not really. It's just my riding gear. I couldn't let on to Jeff anything was up, otherwise he wouldn't have been surprised."

She tipped her head to the side a little and smiled. "It did go off brilliantly, didn't it?"

"Yep."

"He didn't have a clue?"

"Nope." He took her hand in his and led her to a bench sitting on the porch as the party atmosphere around them escalated. Several of the guests on the ranch had been included in the festivities, so it was getting rather crowded and loud as the party got started with the cake and food. His mom and sisters-in-law had done a fantastic job getting everything ready in such a short time without Jeff being the wiser. Leave it to a bunch of women to pull something like this off without the man of the hour knowing anything about it.

Jonathan held Mandy's hand as they rocked in the double rocker. He loved being here like this with her, together without any expectations or anything going on. She watched the proceedings going on around them as he watched her form the corner of his eye. The little smile playing on her lips seemed so like her, he was taken aback by how his heart expanded at the thought of having her in his life. "Do you want to get married?"

"Excuse me?" she said, turning to face him.

"I don't mean right now, but someday, do you want to marry someone?"

She exhaled as the grin reappeared. "Well, yes. I mean, someday, when I know I've found the right guy, I do."

"I know what you mean. I think marriage is in my future too…someday."

She leaned into his shoulder, snuggling a little closer. "This was nice. I'm glad we managed to pull it off."

"You did a fabulous job."

A blush crept up her cheeks. "I didn't do much."

"You helped with the food and cake."

"True, but you kept him occupied and away from the ranch long enough for us to get everything ready."

"All I could do was hope he fell for it. He's a smart man. If he would have guessed something was up, he would have hightailed it out of here."

"You know, I don't think so. He wanted to marry Terri. It's obvious how much in love they are, but he's been burned. His skittishness made him all the more desirable to her, I think. She fell in love with him and wanted him to spend the rest of his life with her. Marriage terrified him, though."

"Yep, but he's in this hook, line, and sinker now."

Someone started up some country music from the stereo in the lodge. One of his favorite artists came on singing about love and how you had to work at it to make it forever. Jonathan climbed to his feet bringing Mandy up with him. "Dance with me, please."

"Of course."

He led her out to the middle of the lawn where they came together perfectly. He liked holding her way too much, he decided, but what the hell. He tucked her into his arms where her head barely reached his shoulder. Her perfume surrounded him as he took a deep breath. He loved how she smelled. The scent drove him to distraction, past the point of reason. "What kind of perfume are you wearing?"

"Nothing special. Just a new perfume I bought recently. Do you like it?"

"I want you to put it in the crease of your thighs next time we make love. I want it surrounding me as I eat your pussy until you scream my name."

"When might this occur, sir?"

"I love when you call me that." He bent his head so he could whisper in her ear. "As soon as we can get away from here."

She shivered in his arms as she tipped her head a little to the side and sighed. God, he loved when she sighed for him. It made him feel powerful and wanted more than anything else in the entire world.

"Will you tie me to the bed again?"

"Maybe. Remember who is in charge here, pet."

"Yes, sir."

He ran his hands up and down her back, soothing her with his touch. Sometimes she acted a bit skittish when they came together, which worried him.

With a glance across the lawn, he caught Peyton's gaze on them. She smiled before winking in his direction. Apparently, his sister-in-law approved of him and Mandy. Good to know, but he still wanted to talk to her, and it probably should be before he and Mandy made love again.

He leaned back in her embrace so he could look into her eyes. "Listen, I need to get a little work done before I cut out for the weekend. How about I meet you at your place in a couple of hours?"

"Should I be wearing something special?"

"Skin, baby, only skin."

A wicked gleam in her eyes promised things he could only imagine as she stepped back, bit her lips, and then licked the bright red surface. His imagination went wild as he thought about those ruby red lips enclosed on his cock as she went down on him.

"Naughty girl."

"Only for you."

"I can't wait."

"I'll see you in a bit then. Don't work too hard."

"I won't."

She raked a fingernail down his chest until she reached the belt buckle at his waist. When the single digit dipped below his waistband, he sucked in a ragged breath and closed his eyes.

The moment the sensation disappeared, he opened his eyes again to see her smiling before she turned and walked away, her hips swaying slightly.

He exhaled on a rush, willing his now hard cock to soften otherwise he would totally embarrass himself as he walked back into the main lodge. *Maybe I should wait a few minutes to talk to Peyton, so she doesn't think I'm some kind of weirdo.*

Too late.

Peyton made her way to his side before he could disappear into the house.

"Hey, cowboy."

"What's up, Peyton?"

"Where did Mandy go?"

"Uh, home, I guess. Why?"

"Well, you two looked pretty chummy. I thought maybe you were going to leave together."

"Why would you think that?"

"I know you're sleeping together, Jonathan. She doesn't keep those kinds of secrets from me."

"So?"

"I'm disappointed is all, I guess."

"We are meeting later. Does that help?"

She grinned a sly, evil little grin. "Yep."

"Uh, can I talk to you a minute in private?"

Now she looked worried. "Yeah. I guess."

She followed him into the house and to his office before he shut the door and turned to face her. "I need to ask you some questions about Mandy." He sat down in his chair, indicating with his hand she should sit in the one opposite him. "You're her best friend so I figured you know her better than anyone."

"I probably do." She folded her hands together in her lap, clutching her fingers tightly. "I don't know whether I can help you though."

"Well, I'm getting the impression she's hiding something. I don't know what and it's bugging me."

"How serious are you about her?"

"I think I'm falling in love with her." He pulled his hat off and raked his fingers through his hair before he put it back on. "I can't get her out of my head. We are great together in bed and she's becoming very special to me, but I fear she's holding back for some reason."

Peyton bit her lip.

"What aren't you telling me, Peyton?"

"I can't talk about it, Jonathan. It's not my place. You need to talk to Mandy."

"Great. Just fucking great."

"Give her time. She's had a rough life."

"What made it so rough? I thought she had a good childhood from what she's told me. She's fairly close to her parents. She got a little wild as a teenager, but nothing major. I don't understand."

"Ask her to be honest with you. Tell her how you feel, Jonathan. If she's feeling the same way, she'll need to explain everything to you. You won't be able to be a couple if she doesn't tell you because it will become a problem at a later date."

"You're being very cryptic."

"I know, but I can't break her confidence." Peyton got to her feet. "I'm sorry. You know I love you. You are family, but she's my best friend."

Peyton disappeared out the door, leaving him to stew in his own thoughts. *Now what the hell am I going to do? What if she won't tell me? What if it's something that could be detrimental to our relationship?*

Jonathan sat in his office until the sun went down, turning the small space dark. The party outside had long ago dispersed, leaving the place in an eerie quiet that made him uncomfortable. Mandy had called several times. Not sure what to think about the conversation he'd had with Peyton, he'd ignored her calls, choosing to think things through before he talked to her.

An Internet search of her name had led to some disturbing information.

He couldn't quite wrap his head around her being arrested for prostitution when she was eighteen. It didn't fit her personality at all. Of course, she probably had been able to pull herself out of that downward spiral of a life. She'd admitted to using drugs when she was younger, but she'd never told him she'd been busted for heroin either. The new picture emerging had him scratching his head. What happened to her in her childhood that led to prostitution and drugs?

A drink sounded really good right now.

He sat in the dark for what seemed like hours as he went over and over in his mind, the information he'd found. A glance at the clock revealed the time. Two am.

His phone rang again. Mandy. His hand hovered over the button, debating on whether to answer and outright ask her about what he'd found, or let it go to voicemail until he could gather his thoughts. He needed to let her explain. It was only fair.

When he picked up his phone and listened to her last message, he really felt like shit.

"Jonathan, it's Mandy again. Please call me when you get this. I'm scared right now and my imagination is running wild with terrifying thoughts. I wanted this to be a special night for us, but now you aren't even talking to me for some reason. Please. God, please, call me. I need you to hold me right now more than anything in the world and tell me we are going to be okay."

She'd hung up after that, leaving him with this hollow feeling in his soul.

Forgiveness was a virtue. What really did he have to forgive her for? It wasn't like this all had happened recently. It had been several years ago, during her wild teenage years, and in all reality, it wasn't fair for him to judge her by her past mistakes. He wasn't perfect by any means, so where did he get off judging her?

His mother tapped on the door as she called out his name. "Jonathan?"

"Come in, Mom."

After she opened the door, she said, "Why are you sitting in the dark at two in the morning, son?"

"I'm thinking. I do it better in the dark."

"About what?"

He sighed heavily as his mother took the seat Peyton had been in several hours before. "I found out some things and I'm not sure how to handle the information."

"What things?"

"Mom, Mandy was arrested at eighteen for prostitution and drugs, heroin to be exact."

"Oh, honey."

"I know. Shocking, right?"

"Not really."

"Why not really?"

"Jonathan, I knew about Mandy's record a long time ago. When she first started, she told me about it because you know we do a background check on everyone who works here. She explained the circumstances of her arrest then. I understand why she did what she did."

"Explain it to me, Mom, because I sure don't get it."

"I can't, son. She needs to tell you herself."

He jumped to his feet, sending his chair crashing to the floor behind him. "What the fuck?"

"Don't talk to me like that."

"Sorry, but I don't understand why everyone is keeping stuff from me. How can I think about being in love with her if no one will tell me what is going on?"

Nina got to her feet and took her son in a big hug. "Jonathan, it's her place to tell you. Have you told her you love her?"

"No."

"Then that's the first step. If she loves you too, then she'll tell you about her past. It's not my place to break her confidence."

Nina silently walked out of his office, shutting the door behind her.

Jonathan paced the floor several times before he grabbed his keys, his wallet, and his hat, and walked out.

Within minutes, he was headed down the road toward Bandera. He was going to get some answers to his questions if it was the last thing he did. If their relationship survived the night, they would probably survive anything.

* * * *

Mandy stared at her phone after her last call to Jonathan. Her heart hurt as she wrapped her arms around her middle and sank down on the couch. She didn't know what to think anymore. He'd been so loving earlier at Terri and Jeff's wedding when they had danced, but now he wasn't taking her calls.

She pressed her lips together to hold back the tears. Falling in love with him, deeper than anything she'd ever felt before, hurt really bad. She didn't understand why he'd turned his back on her, but he apparently had.

A soft knock brought her to her feet as she wiped away the trickle of a tear on her face. She sniffed a couple of times, trying desperately to clear her nose before she looked to see who had dropped by. She peeked out the peephole, surprised to find Jonathan in front of her door.

Not sure what to expect, she unlocked the top lock and then the bottom one before she opened it.

"Hey."

"Hi."

"Can I come in?"

"Uh, yeah, I guess so." She stepped back, allowing his big frame to step around her. After she shut the door, she turned to face him as she rubbed her bare arms to calm the chills. "You were supposed to come over several hours ago."

"I know."

"How come you didn't answer my calls?" she asked, as she took a seat across from him. Right now it didn't seem like a good idea to sit next to him. "I called several times."

"I know, and I'm sorry."

He looked nervous, edgy, and uncomfortable. Why, she wondered. "Jonathan, what's going on? You seem so distant right now when you weren't earlier. What have I done to displease you?"

"I need to ask you some questions, and I'm trying to think of how to word them without pissing you off."

She got a sinking feeling in the pit of her stomach. Something wasn't right here, and the thought of what he was getting at terrified her. "Okay."

"Will you tell me the truth?"

Somehow, that made her suspicion worse. "If I can, but there are things in my past I won't discuss, even with you."

"That doesn't make me feel better, Mandy."

"I'm sorry. I can't talk about them." She rubbed her arms again. "There are some things better left buried."

He took his hat off, sitting it on the arm of the chair before he faced her again. "I did an Internet search on you and I found something out that's bothering me."

"You did what?"

"An Internet search. You know. It brings up past records and things like that."

She jumped to her feet, rage rolling through her at his audacity. "You son of a bitch! What's in my past is in my past. You didn't even ask me, you just went on the fucking web and searched. How dare you!"

"I had to. I knew you were hiding something from me. Will you tell me why you were arrested for prostitution and heroin possession? I need to understand, Mandy."

"Get out! I don't want to see you again. Do you hear me? Never. Don't talk to me, don't call me, don't touch me!"

He stood and reached out his hand, but she slapped it away. "I said don't touch me. I hate you! Do you hear me? I hate everything about your fucking perfect life. You've never done a damned thing wrong, I'm sure, and it shows. You and your perfect family. No one is good enough for you. Go find some good little girl who's never done a damned thing wrong, never been in a situation where she had to do something to survive."

He came closer, trying to draw her into his arms. "Mandy, talked to me. Don't shut me out."

She pushed him away with her hands on his chest, ignoring the way her palms and fingers tingled from the contact. "I said go." Tears streamed down her cheeks now, but she was unable to stop them, even for him. "Just go," she whispered, broken, body and soul.

The soft snick of the door echoed in the small apartment as she sank to the floor.

Chapter Eleven

Days went by, turning into weeks, and then months. Christmas came and went including the beautiful wedding of Jackson and Samantha.

Jonathan had tried to contact her on several occasions, but she'd let his calls go to voicemail. She couldn't see them together anymore, not with her past. Moving on seemed the best option.

Mandy didn't attend even though it hurt her not to. Samantha was her friend.

She'd quit the ranch right after the blow up with Jonathan. When she'd talked to Nina and told her what happened, she'd understood even though she suggested telling him the truth about her past. Mandy couldn't. Her whole messed up life was her fault, she knew. The rape, the drug possession, and the prostitution arrest. Everything was her fault, exactly how her parents had told her all those years ago.

Summer would be here soon. After graduating from her courses in June, she could move on to somewhere else outside of Bandera.

The girls on the ranch didn't understand either since she wouldn't tell them what happened between her and Jonathan, only that they had a disagreement, and no, they weren't seeing each other anymore. Only Peyton and Nina knew the truth.

She looked in the mirror as she put on her makeup to cover up the dark circles under her eyes. Sleep eluded her most nights these days, except for the reoccurring nightmare of reliving the rape in her dreams. Nothing seemed to erase those feelings of helplessness anymore, not even talking to Peyton.

Maybe professional help would make it easier for her to deal with this. She could try, she guessed. It wouldn't hurt.

As soon as she'd finished putting on her makeup, she grabbed her purse and keys before she headed toward the door to go to class. At least that kept her occupied for a few hours each day. The rest of the time, she couldn't concentrate on anything besides the feelings of loneliness and worthlessness that were a constant blanket of guilt.

A guy in one of her classes approached her as she sat outside trying to study for their upcoming exam.

"Hi there."

She glanced up, catching the reflection off his sunglasses. She shielded her eyes from the glare. "Hi." She'd seen him in a few of her classes, they'd exchanged greetings a few times, but weren't friends by any stretch of the imagination.

"Can I join you?"

"Uh, sure. I guess."

"You're Mandy, right?"

"Yes, and you are?"

"Brandon."

"Nice to meet you."

"You too."

The silence stretched for a moment while she tried to figure out why he'd come over in the first place. It wasn't like she'd talked to him before or even really noticed him, for that matter. He was kind of cute in a boyish kind of way, but not the rugged type she enjoyed. "Is there something I can help you with?"

"Yeah. I think so. How about a cup of coffee?"

"You know, I don't think that's such a good idea."

"Why not? Are you seeing someone?"

Despair threatened to choke her as she thought about Jonathan. "No, not really."

"Then you should be free for coffee, right?"

"Why are you being so persistent about this?"

"I think you're cute. I've watched you during class."

Okay, that's kind of weird.

"Come on. It's just coffee. Please?"

What the hell. It's just coffee, right? "All right."

"Fantastic. There's a shop around the corner." Brandon stood and held out his hand to help her to her feet. "Maybe we can brainstorm a bit about this exam coming up. I'm kind of lost on the subject matter."

She laughed a little, and it was a good feeling. It wasn't something she'd done much of over the last few months. "I know what you mean." She grabbed her backpack from the table, slipping her book in through the zippered pouch before closing it and slinging it over her shoulder.

They walked side-by-side down the concrete walkway to the edge of the street and turned left. The coffee shop sat one block down. She'd been there frequently over the last few years of attending classes at the college, so she knew the owners and most of the employees by first name.

The bell dinged when they went through the door to find a table. The only empty one in the whole place sat near the back. The red upholstered seats were cool to the back of her thighs where her bare skin touched when she slid into the booth. Fifties music played on the overhead speaker system. It reminded her of an old diner like they had during the run on Happy Days on television.

The waitress stopped at their table, taking a pen from behind her ear to write down their order. "What can I get'cha?"

"Coffee please. Cream and sugar?"

"You, sir?"

"Same."

"Be right back."

When the woman left them, Mandy glanced across the table right into the green eyes of the man who had asked her for coffee. "I'm sorry. What did you say your name was?"

"Brandon. Brandon Gilliand."

Her world went dark. *What the fuck?* "Uh, where did you say you're from?"

"Minnesota. Why?" He grabbed her hand from across the table. "Are you okay? You're very pale."

"Yeah," she squeaked. "I, uh—" *Oh God. He can't be related. Surely he's not related to that motherfucker I would kill if I could get my hands on him.*

"Mandy?"

She took several deeps breaths to calm her racing heart. No way could he have found her, right? It's just coincidence. She cleared her throat. "Sorry. You remind me of someone, that's all."

"Obviously someone you aren't fond of by the look on your face."

No way could she explain how now that she looked at him, really looked at him, he reminded her of Matt Gilliand, the man who'd rape her as a fifteen-year-old child. "Not really, no."

"Care to explain?" His cell phone rang in his pocket. "Let me grab this. It's my dad, and it might be important." He punched the screen on his phone. "Hey, Dad. What's up?"

The voice on the other end of the phone had memories rushing back in a spiraling kaleidoscope of colors making her stomach roll with nausea.

It's okay for me to touch you, Mandy. You are a special girl to me. I won't hurt you. You'll like it, I promise.

She jumped to her feet, sprinting for the door. The moment she hit the edge of the sidewalk, she threw up into the gutter. Her body shook as she tried breathing through her nose to calm her stomach. Her world tilted sideways.

Strong hands gripped her shoulders, pulling her hair out of her face. "It's okay, baby. I'm here."

"Jonathan?" she asked, her gaze swimming with tears as she looked up into the familiar eyes of the man she loved. Where had he come from? Was he following her? "What are you doing here?" She quickly wiped her face with her hand. He handed her a handkerchief. "Thank you."

"You're welcome. You okay?"

"Yes." She shook her head as the tears returned. "No."

He pulled her into his arms as she broke down in gut-wrenching sobs that rocked her entire frame. "Ssh. It's okay. I won't let anything hurt you." With his arm around her shoulders, he led her to his truck parked a few feet down the road.

The guy she'd been about to have coffee with came up behind them carrying the backpack she'd left in the booth and handed it to her. "Mandy? Are you okay?"

"I'm fine, Brandon. I'm sorry, but I won't be able to have coffee with you." She noticed he took a long look at Jonathan before he nodded and turned away.

"New boyfriend?"

"No. He's in one of my classes. He asked me out for coffee."

"And that made you throw up in the gutter?"

She pressed her lips together as his image swam in front of her.

"Mandy, honey, I can't help you if you won't tell me what's going on." With a gentle hand, he pushed her hair off her forehead and pressed a kiss there.

"I can't. You'll hate me. Everyone will blame me, just like my parents did. It was all my fault. Everything was my fault." Hiccups wracked her body as he opened the door on the truck and lifted her like a child into the seat before he shut the door.

Her body shuddered as she pressed her hands between her knees.

When he got into the driver's seat, he turned the ignition key, the engine roaring to life. They pulled away from the curb and drove down the street, headed for where, she didn't know. Right now, she didn't care.

Why had he been in San Antonio near the college? Was he following her? What if he knew about her past and now he hated her enough to hurt her? She shook her head. Jonathan would never do anything to harm her, not in a million years. But that still left the unanswered question of why he was there?

Her voice came out in a whisper. "Where are we going?"

"Some place where we can talk."

Crap. Now he wants answers again.

Scenery went by in a blur as they drove out of town back toward Bandera. It didn't surprise her that he would take her back toward home. It was what he knew and was comfortable with.

Silence enveloped them during the forty-five minute ride.

Terror gripped her. What the hell would she tell him as to why she'd lost it outside the coffee shop? She couldn't possibly tell him the truth. He would never understand and he would blame her just like her parents had, for everything.

When they drove on past Thunder Ridge's gate, she got confused. Even though she'd been on the ranch for several years, she'd never really ventured down the road past the gates. The road turned from blacktop to gravel as he continued on. Fences still lined the road, telling her there were ranches even down this far.

Soon, he turned off on a side road that went up and over the hill toward the right. Deer sprang out of the bushes, crossing in front of the bumper of the truck. Jonathan never said a word.

They crested a hill before he pulled off near a metal gate with a huge lock to keep anyone from roaming onto the property without permission.

When he got out and unlocked the gate, she figured it was probably Thunder Ridge property and he was taking her somewhere private.

Good. If she lost him to the memories bombarding her, it wouldn't be in front of his family.

He locked the gate back up as soon as they pulled through and then jumped back inside the truck to continue on until they were at the top of one of the hills overlooking the area. Bluebonnets blanketed the landscape this time of year, giving the hillside a bright blue splash of color.

"How beautiful."

"Yes, you are."

She glanced his way and blushed. "Not me, silly, the hillside."

"You put the landscape to shame."

"You're a charmer."

"Stating the truth, darlin'."

She pulled the visor down in front of her face, to check how badly her makeup had smeared when she puked in the gutter. "Wow. Yeah, I'm beautiful with all this mascara under my eyes." She searched in his glove box for a tissue or napkin she could wipe her face with. "Ah. Found one." She wiped the black from beneath her eyes until she was satisfied that she no longer looked like a raccoon. "Better."

"Do you want to tell me what that was all about back there?"

"I wish I could."

In a complete bout of rage not like him at all, he punch his fist against the dashboard of his truck, breaking the skin on his knuckles.

"Jesus, Jonathan." She grabbed for his hand to wipe the blood from his skin. "Are you nuts?"

"No, I'm fucking frustrated as all hell, Mandy. I've been going crazy trying to figure out what the hell happened between us."

She dabbed at the skin until the blood was gone. She shrugged when he pulled his hand back. "We broke up."

"No, you shut me out."

She closed her eyes for a moment before opening them again to meet his gaze. "Yeah, I guess I did."

"Why?"

"Because there are things in my past you are better off not knowing, and when you snooped into my police record to find out some things, it pissed me off. I wanted to be the perfect girl for you like your family wants and like you want, but I can't be that."

"I don't want a Barbie doll, Mandy. I wanted you. I still do."

"How, Jonathan? How can you say that?"

"Because I love you, you crazy woman. I haven't been able to get you out of my mind no matter how hard I try. You are a part of my heart that can't be replaced, no matter how far you go or how much you shut me out."

"You love me?"

He scooted to the center of the seat, unbuckled her seat belt, and took her face in his hands. "Yes, I love you."

Fresh tears streamed down her cheeks. She had no idea how someone so perfect could be in love with her, but she wasn't going to question his feelings or her own anymore. She had to tell him the truth about her past. It wasn't a matter of him turning his back on her now. If he did, it would hurt like nothing she'd ever felt before, but maybe, just maybe, he would understand.

"I love you too."

He grasped her to his chest and whispered, "Thank you, God."

When he moved back so she could see his face, she was surprised to see tears in his own eyes.

"You mean everything to me."

"I hope you'll continue to love me when I tell you about my past."

"Honey, it doesn't matter. What's in the past is just that, in the past."

"I still have to tell you for my own piece of mind. There can be no more secrets between us."

"I'm glad to hear you say that."

She closed her eyes as she bent her head. "I had a baby at fifteen. I gave her up for adoption because my parents wouldn't let me keep her. I don't know where she is, but I would like to find her someday."

"I'm sure it was something you regret every day."

"It is, but there is more. I was raped. It resulted in my pregnancy. My parents didn't believe me when I told them about it because it was my stepfather's brother. He was twenty years older than me at the time and visiting us for Christmas. He came into my room and forced himself on me. He mocked me, said if I told anyone they wouldn't believe me, but I still told my parents. He was right. They thought I was lying to cover up sleeping with someone in my class. When the pregnancy was discovered, they forced me to have her and give her up."

"Oh, baby. I'm so sorry you've had to deal with this for all this time." He grasped her face in his hands, forcing her to look into his eyes. "Listen to me, Mandy. You were fifteen. It wasn't your fault."

"But he said I made him do it. He said I was pretty, and he couldn't help himself."

"Mandy, he was the adult. He is responsible, not you. You did nothing wrong, honey. In fact, I will help you if you want to bring charges against him."

"I…I don't know if I can."

"It's up to you, but I hope you think about it for yourself and your daughter. You need closure."

"There's more."

"Go ahead."

"Yes, I was arrested for prostitution and drugs when I was eighteen. I left home in a hurry when I finished high school and had to live on the streets for a while since I had no job and no money. I got in with the wrong crowd. I ended up having sex for money and getting busted for drugs. I didn't take them, but I had heroin in my possession when they arrested me on the streets. I was dealing at the same time I was prostituting myself." She exhaled and tipped her head back on her shoulders. "God, I feel like such a fool."

"You were a kid trying to make it on your own. We all make mistakes."

"Not you, not the perfect Young family."

"Mandy, you have no idea the things some of my brothers and I have gotten into over the years. We've barely managed to keep ourselves out of jail on plenty of occasions."

"Really?"

"Yes. Ask my mother. She'll tell you all about it."

Mandy couldn't help but smile a little thinking about the nine of them getting into trouble with their parents. Obviously, it hadn't been that bad or they would have a record. Of course, she had no idea if any of them did or not, but it was nice to know they weren't perfect either.

"I need to tell you one more thing because it might change how you feel about me."

"Nothing will change the way I feel."

"Don't say that until you've heard this."

"Okay. Go ahead."

"I can't have children."

"Why?"

"The pregnancy and birth did so much damage to my insides that I can't carry a baby to term anymore. There is way too much scar tissue in my uterus."

"It's okay."

"No, it's not, Jonathan. You want children. You told me as much. You want a big family like your parents had, and I can't give that to you."

"Mandy, listen to me. I would like children, yes, but that doesn't mean I wouldn't love any child we had together whether we are the biological parents or not. We can adopt or look into other options."

"You'd do that?"

"Yes, ma'am. There are plenty of kids out there who need parents that don't have any. I wouldn't have any trouble loving a child like that."

"How did I get so lucky to find you?"

"You corralled me a long time ago, sweetheart. The moment I saw you with Peyton, I knew you were someone special. It just took me a few years to figure out how special."

"I love you, Jonathan."

"I love you too, baby."

He slowly lowered his head so he could take her mouth in a soft, soul-stealing kiss. The moment he lifted his head, she knew this was it. He was the one she'd been destined to find, the one who could heal her tattered heart, hold it in the palm of his hand, and forever be the cowboy she could call her own.

Chapter Twelve

Darkness fell around them as they laid in the bed of his truck looking up at the stars over their heads.

After their talk, they climbed into the back, spread out the blanket he produced from behind the seats, and she'd laid her head on his chest.

His heartbeat steady and strong, something she knew she would forever hold in her heart. He loved her. It was something that would take a lifetime for her to comprehend, but he did love her.

His fingers did a slow crawl up and down her arm, leaving goose bumps in their wake. Tingles spread from where he touched her to every part of her body. From the moment he'd laid his hands on her, she'd been putty in his grasp.

"I love you," he whispered against her hair, before he kissed the top of her head.

"I love you and just for the record, I will never get tired of hearing that so you can say it all you want."

A rumble of laughter echoed beneath her ear. "Good to know, baby girl."

A coyote howled in the distance. Leaves rustled in the night breeze over their heads as the temperature began to drop.

She shivered.

"Are you cold?"

"A little."

"Want me to warm you up?"

"How do you plan to go about doing that, cowboy?"

"I have my ways, little lady." He moved so he was now over her as he began to kiss his way from her forehead, down over her eyelids, across her cheek, until he reached her right ear. "I'm going to make you come so hard, you'll see stars."

"Promises, promises."

"Remember that when you are begging me to let you come."

His teeth nipped at her earlobe, bringing awareness to her whole body as he continued his journey down her neck, nibbling as he went.

"Sit up," he said moving so she could rise. Her t-shirt whipped over her head, leaving her in her lacy pink bra. "I do love your undergarments. They are so sexy." He ran his tongue along the each cup of her bra where they laid against her breasts.

Her nipples pulled into tight nubs, rubbing against the fabric of her bra in the most erotic way she could ever have imagined.

He avoided moving the cups out of his way as he continued down her abdomen until he reached the waist of her jeans. "Lie back now."

She got comfortable on her back as he worked the button loose on her pants and removed them along with her underwear in one swish of fabric. Cool night air wafted over her skin, making her shiver or was it the anticipation of his touch? She wasn't sure anymore. "Touch me."

"I will. In a minute, but for right now, I want to look."

She could almost feel his gaze on her skin.

"You are magnificent. All soft, glowing, and ready for me."

His hands were rough on her flesh, the calluses erotically abrasive. He took her foot in his hand and brought it to his mouth, kissing and nipping as he moved up the inside of her leg. Her pussy wept with the need to have him touch her there, with his tongue, with his mouth, with his fingers. Hell, she didn't care. She just needed him to do something besides this erotic, slow seduction he was hell-bent on performing. "Jonathan, please."

"Oh, I love when you beg, my beautiful woman."

His mouth moved to the other foot as she sighed in frustration. He would be the death of her before the night was over if he didn't hurry up.

When she felt the warm puff of air on her clit, she almost came straight up off the bed of the truck. "Yes."

He brushed his mouth against her inner thigh, and she almost smacked him in the head for avoiding the point where she ached for him. But when he returned to lick her clit once, then twice, she opened her thighs farther and scrunched her eyes closed as she waited with bated breath. Her climax would be fast and furious when it broke over her.

He licked slowly, bringing her up a miniscule degree at a time. Her legs began to shake as she hovered on the edge of climax for several moments, waiting for him to tell her it was okay for her to come. She held her breath, afraid to breathe until he whispered the words.

Finally, he whispered, "Come for me, Mandy."

Her world exploded in a shower of flashing lights as she screamed his name to the wind. "Jonathan!"

He continued to slowly lick her as her heart and breathing returned to a semi-normal rate and she began to shiver from the chill in the air, or her body ramping up again, she wasn't sure.

"I'll be right back. There is another blanket in the truck."

When he returned moments later, he carried a wool blanket in his hands as he hopped back up in the bed of the truck. He covered her body with it, letting her catch her breath and warm herself up before things progressed to the next step. "I wish it was a little warmer. I would spread you out on that bed of grass over there, make you come several more times, and then fuck you into tomorrow."

"We'll save that for something to do in a couple of months." She giggled as he moved up beside her.

"I'm glad you are thinking of a future for us."

"I love you. I want to be with you."

He twisted a strand of her hair around his finger before bringing it to his lips and rubbing it across the surface. "I love you too."

His eyes darkened in the cab light over their heads. "What's wrong?"

"I'm hard and achy for you, but there are a couple of things we need to get out in the open."

Her stomach knotted as she tried to think of what he might be talking about. She'd been honest with him, telling about the rape, her daughter, and the arrests. What else could he want to talk about? "Make love to me, Jonathan. We can talk afterward."

"No. We need to talk now before things go any further."

She waited not so patiently as he continued to run his gaze over her face.

"What happened earlier when I found you outside the coffee shop? Why were you throwing up in the gutter?"

"I told you there was a guy from my class who asked me out for coffee. It turns out he is the son of the man who raped me."

"Oh shit."

She tucked the blanket around her and sat up, determined to clear the air now that she knew he loved her and wouldn't leave her alone. "Yeah. I'm terrified that he's found me. I didn't even know he had children. That makes the whole thing really gross, not that it wasn't before. He has a son that is about the same age I am."

"You don't have to worry, honey. I won't let him hurt you ever again."

"I know you won't." She leaned back against the bed of the truck as she gazed into the eyes of the man she loved. They'd come a long way in a short time, learning to love each other and accept the differences between them, but loving each other through whatever came would be the trick of a lifetime. "Why were you near the coffee shop anyway?"

"I came to find you. I got your class schedule from Peyton. I figured it was time we talked and cleared the air. You are important to me."

He moved to her side and pulled her into his embrace, her head on his chest. She could feel the steady beat of his heart beneath her cheek. The slow rise and fall of his chest when he breathed made her feel calm and safe. He did that for her without even trying. "You are the best thing that's ever happened to me, and I'm trying to figure out why I deserve you."

"Because you're a special woman. You're always doing things for other people. You care about others more than yourself and it shows. We are good together, you and I."

She grasped the button at the top of his shirt, slowing going down each one in turn until she could push the material aside. His chest was sprinkled with dark chair that she loved to bury her fingers in. She let her hand smooth over the muscles of his pecs before she ran a fingernail over his left nipple.

He shuddered in response to her touch.

When she let her hand wander down his abdomen to the belt buckle at his waist, she slowly undid it, leaving it hanging loose as she reached for his button. His breath hitched as she parted the material, letting his cock spring free. He was commando.

"No underwear? You naughty boy."

He groaned as she ran her fingernail down his bulging cock.

She sat up, letting the blanket hang loose as she moved down and grasped his jeans at the hips to pull them off. She wanted to taste him, breathe in his scent, and bring him pleasure beyond what he'd ever felt before.

After she got his jeans down around his ankles, she licked her way up his thigh until she could bury her nose in the crease between his balls and his leg. His scent drove her wild with need. It was somewhere between musk and man.

She ran her tongue around the base of his balls. His moan of satisfaction made her smile against his skin. The little sounds he made when they made love, made her heart sing with joy. She did that for him, only her.

The moment she licked from his balls to the tip of his cock, he lifted his hips in silent invitation to take him in her mouth. She circled the head, once, twice, before she slipped him between her lips. The small amount of suction she applied to the head pulled a guttural sound from deep in his throat.

He fisted her hair, guiding her to what he wanted.

With her mouth encircling his cock, she pushed downward until she felt the head bump against the back of her throat, and her nose was buried in the hair at the base of his cock. She worked her throat a couple of times, bringing a primitive noise from his mouth she'd never heard before.

She loved to make him loose control and this blow job was doing the trick.

Jonathan pulled at her hair, forcing her to release his cock from her mouth. "Stop, Mandy, or I'll come in your mouth when I want to be buried in your pussy." He pulled her up his chest and rolled her over onto her back. "Do I need to continue to use a condom?"

"I don't think so. We are exclusive, right?"

"Yes, ma'am."

"Then no. I think we're good. I haven't been with anyone but you in quite a while."

"I've been celibate myself for about eighteen months before we had sex."

The head of his cock bumped against her pussy lips, slowly parting her so he could bury himself to the hilt. Giving him a blow job had ramped up her own desire to almost explosive, doing almost as much for her as it did for him.

When he slowly pushed inside her pussy, she wet her finger in her mouth before she reached down to encircle her clit.

"Watching you masturbate is really hot." He looked down to where their bodies met. "Make yourself really wet for me." He continued to slowly sink inside her until he was fully buried. He shuddered as he closed his eyes.

The view was perfection. He'd braced himself on his hands so as not to put too much weight on her chest. His arms bulged from the strain of holding himself still while he unhurriedly rocked his hips. His head was tipped back on his shoulders, his face intense with concentration. She could tell he was absorbing every slick slide of his cock inside her, feeling each ripple of her pussy around him, and enjoying every sensation going through his body.

The sight of him loosing himself to her, made her need spiral out of control. Her orgasm hovered on the edge of her consciousness as she worked her clit with her fingers. The need to come overwhelmed her to the point where she had to grit her teeth to keep it under control. She pinched herself with her left hand to stop the oncoming tide of pleasure, making it recede back slightly so she wouldn't come before he told her she could.

"You feel fantastic. So wet. So tight." He thrust several more times. "I could fuck you all night."

"Jonathan?"

"Yeah?"

"I'm hurting. I need to come so badly, I ache."

"Only when I say you can, not before."

She groaned as she closed her eyes and tried to think of something, anything that would forestall the roll of the orgasm. She whimpered, the sound a high cry of need she couldn't control.

His thrusts began to increase in intensity and speed. Her head felt like it was about to detonate from the tight rein she held on her climax.

His breathing became ragged. His thrusting rhythm became disjointed as he continued to bury himself inside her.

"I'm so there, Jonathan. Please, let me come."

He opened his eyes and looked down into her face. The love shining in his gaze brought tears to her eyes. She'd never seen something so precious and beautiful in her life.

"Come for me, Mandy. Milk me dry."

Her climax washed over her like waves breaking on the shores, exploding in shards of color so brilliant, she couldn't see beyond the rainbow. She cried out his name as she wrapped her legs around his hips and brought them tighter together.

He shuddered as he came inside her, his own climax enough to cause him to collapse on her chest, his nose buried in her hair. His breath came out in harsh pants, hot against her ear.

She wrapped her arms around his back, holding him close to her heart. He'd earned every piece, heart, body, and soul. There was no way she could deny her feelings for him. He was a part of her now, forever.

* * * *

Jonathan peeked into the window of the jewelry shop in downtown San Antonio, checking out the sparkling diamonds in the pretty settings. He had in mind what he wanted for

Mandy, but he hadn't been able to find it yet. It needed to be special, like her, but not gaudy. He decided to go inside and see what they might have in the case before he moved onto the next shop.

It had been several weeks now since he'd told her he loved her and she returned his feelings tenfold. They spent many a night making love, talking, laughing, and loving each other beyond anything he'd ever felt, and he knew it was time to make things official. He wanted to ask her to marry him.

Graduation was a week off for her. She would finally have her degree and then she needed to figure out what to do from there. He'd told her if she wanted to move to Houston, he would move with her. He could do the marketing and website remotely for Thunder Ridge if need be. Maybe come back to the ranch once a month or something to catch up on things that needed to be done or to meet with his parents about new items requiring addition to the plan. It would work, he knew it would. It all depended on where she wanted to go to get a job. He'd follow her anywhere, even if it meant leaving Thunder Ridge.

After all, he was an adult and needed to find his own way in life with her by his side.

"May I help you?"

"Yes, sir. I'm looking for an engagement ring for my girlfriend."

"Very good, sir. I have a whole case of settings over here that you might be interested in looking at. Of course, if you would like to design your own, that's an option too. We can set any diamond in whatever you might come up with."

"I hadn't thought of designing my own. Thank you for bringing that up, but I would still like to see what you have."

"Of course." The white haired man moved down to a case to Jonathan's right. "These are the settings we have. Take your time. Look over each one. If there is something you would like to see more closely, let me know."

"Thank you."

The man moved back down to the other cases, shifting things around to show them better to the customers as Jonathan looked over the pieces in the case. There were several he liked, but nothing seemed to be exactly right.

One caught his attention as he leaned closer to see inside the case better. It was a square cut diamond in a simple band with smaller diamonds surrounding it as well as along the band itself. The gold swirled up and around the center diamond, reminding him of something he'd seen in her apartment, a painting of horses running along a stream and the swirl of dandelions as the horses moved past. The white puffs of the flowers were spotted all over the painting making it almost look like snow. "May I see that one?"

"Certainly, sir." The man unlocked the case, brought the ring box out, and handed it to Jonathan. "It's a two carat center diamond with the smaller round cut diamonds on the band. Total weight on the ring itself is three carats. It was a special design for a lady here in town by her fiancé, but they broke up before he gave it to her."

"It's gorgeous."

"It is beautiful, yes, and very special. There isn't another one like it."

"How much?" Jonathan about choked when he was told the total, but after he thought about it for a minute, he knew Mandy was worth every penny. "I'll take it."

"Very good, sir. Do you know your ladies ring size? I can have it sized accordingly and have it ready by Friday."

"I don't at the moment, but give me a minute and I'll find out." He pulled out his cell phone and hit Peyton's number.

"Hey, you."

"Hi, Peyton. Listen, I have a question for you, but you can't let on that you know anything, all right?"

"Sure. What's up?"

"I'm buying Mandy a ring, but I don't know her size. Do you?"

"Yep. I bought her a ring last year for Christmas. She wears a seven."

He smiled and nodded to the gentleman across the counter. "Perfect. Thank you."

"You bet. I hope it's gorgeous. She's a special lady."

"Don't I know it. Thanks again." He hung up his phone, grabbed his wallet, and handed over his credit card. Yes, she was worth every penny and then some.

That evening while he laid in bed holding her to his side as she slept on his chest, he ran his hands down her arm, loving the feel of her skin beneath his fingers. She smelled like flowers and woman, the woman he loved, and he couldn't help the smile that played on his lips. Everything about her fit him so perfectly he was almost scared to wonder what their life would be like together.

She rolled away from him, tucking the pillow under her face. The curve of her bare back was beautiful. He couldn't help but reach out to run his fingers down her spine until he reached the swell of her buttocks. They'd made love already tonight, but he wanted her again. When his hand reached her butt cheek, he smoothed his palm over the surface. She moaned softly in her sleep but didn't awaken.

Her legs were parted slightly, with one knee in front of the other, leaving her pussy open to his touch. He slowly penetrated her pussy with one finger, feeling her wetness on his hand. She widened her legs a little, giving him more access even though her breathing told him she still slept.

Good God, she's wet and ready for me.

He pushed two fingers into her, slowly pumping them in and out, as her hips began to move with his rhythm. He trailed his lips up her back to the nape of her neck, nipping at the skin of her shoulder.

"Are you going to tease me forever or are you going to fuck me?"

He smiled against her skin. "Do you want me to fuck you?"

"Hell yea, you silly man." He pulled his fingers out as she rolled back toward him. "You were giving me a really nice dream, but now that I'm awake, I want the real thing."

"You looked so sexy lying there with your back to me. Your ass is just begging to be fucked."

"Is that a promise?"

"You bet, sweetheart, but I'm going to eat you out first, until you're crying out wanting to come."

"You can be a real bastard, you know that?"

"Yep." He smiled as he settled himself between her thighs, and began a slow, thorough job of bringing her to the brink of insanity. He licked around her clit and then down the slit before he wriggled his tongue inside her pussy as she moaned softly. "You taste good."

"Quit talking and lick me."

"Demanding woman." He laughed a little before he did his best to give her what she wanted without actually giving her an orgasm. He would torture her a little and then give her the pleasure she sought with his cock. She'd climaxed before with him in her ass, but he'd brought a surprise to the table tonight she hadn't seen yet. A nice little clit bullet waited in the bedside table, for just this moment.

When she was to the point her hips, legs, and abdomen quivered with the need to come, he sat up, rolled her over, and grabbed the bullet vibrator as well as the lube from the nightstand drawer. He dribbled the slick, wet substance down the crack of her ass, slicking her and himself up so it wouldn't be uncomfortable for her. "I have a surprise for you."

"Oh?"

"Yep. Here." He flipped on the vibrator and handed it to her. "Put it on your clit."

She reached between her legs, placing it right on her clit. "Oh fuck."

"Nice, eh?"

"Holy hell, that's good."

He pushed the head of his cock through the tight muscles of her ass, shuddering at the sensations bombarding him from all sides. The slick channel hugged him like a glove on a cold winter day, making it almost impossible for him not to push farther faster. He could feel the vibrator as he slowly pushed deeper. The vibrations zipped along his cock, before settling in his balls, and then sizzling along his spine. He knew he wouldn't last long at this rate, but the sounds she was making below him told him she wouldn't last long either.

"Oh God, oh God, oh God."

She spread her thighs farther apart, taking him even deeper.

"I can't hold on."

"I'm right there. Push harder. Faster. I'll go off like a rocket."

He picked up his pace, fucking her with increasing speed and thrust. The bed bounced hard against the wall as they fucked like bunnies.

Snap!

"What the hell?"

A burse of laughter echoed in the small room as the bed frame split, sending them crashing down onto the floor, him still buried in her ass. "Shit. We broke the bed."

He couldn't help himself from joining her as they laughed so loud, Joey banged on the wall beside them.

"You two want to keep in down in there? Good God!"

They continued to laugh until he sobered enough to remove his now soft cock from her backside. He walked into the bathroom, coming back with a warm washcloth to clean her up.

She hadn't moved, but continued to giggle as she buried her face in the pillow.

He wiped her pussy and ass free of the lube, before tossing the wet cloth onto the dresser.

"I guess I can truly say you are the man for me. You broke a bed for me."

With a shake of his head, rolled her over, and helped her get to her feet. "Where are we going to sleep now?"

"My place, I guess."

"We need to talk about that."

"Talk about what?"

"Where you are going to live. Of course, now that you've broken my bed, we will have to sleep on yours until we can get another one, a nice one, a bigger one."

"I don't care where we sleep, as long as you are beside me."

"Good answer." He kissed her nose. "I love you, Mandy."

"I love you too."

He pulled on his jeans and then slipped on a t-shirt as she gathered up her clothes and began to put them on. "Are you hungry?"

"Yeah, a little."

"How about we go into town and grab a burger?"

"Sounds good."

A few minutes later, they were bouncing along the dirt road toward the gate of Thunder Ridge. Miller's Burger Shack in Bandera was the perfect place to get a burger this late at night. The bar crowd and the high school kids usually hung out there every weekend, but since it was Tuesday, there shouldn't be too many people around.

When they pulled up in front of the place, Mandy sighed. "I love this place."

"Me too. I used to hang out here a lot after school."

She smiled and winked. "Did you buy some pretty girl milkshakes?"

He brought her hand to his mouth, kissing her fingers one by one until she was breathless. "Nope. The woman I wanted wasn't here yet."

"You are such a gentleman."

"I try."

They climbed out of the truck, meeting in the front as they clasped hands and headed for the door. He loved the thought of being with her forever. She was the perfect fit to his other half.

After they went through the door, she stopped dead in her tracks, her face sheet white.

"Mandy?"

"It's him."

Chapter Thirteen

"Who?"

She shivered as she tried to get closer to Jonathan. *How did he find me?* "The man who raped me."

"Are you sure?" Jonathan asked, as he wrapped his arm around her and pulled her closer to his side.

"I'll never forget his face, Jonathan, or his voice telling me he wouldn't hurt me and it would be okay for him to touch me."

"Do you want to leave?"

She closed her eyes and tried to focus. The man had no control over her anymore and it was time for her to face her fear of him. She wasn't the one at fault for what he'd done, he was. She had been a child, a young girl coming into her own, when he'd stolen her innocence away from her. "No." She pulled in a deep breath and opened her eyes. Brandon sat across the booth from him. "I'm not going to let him hurt me anymore."

"Good girl."

They walked forward, moving past the booth where they sat, so they could take a seat farther down. She could feel his gaze on her, but she refused to acknowledge his existence. He was nothing to her.

"Mandy?" Brandon called to her as they sat down. "Hey."

"Hi, Brandon."

"Uh, it's nice to see you. Do you live here in Bandera?"

"Yes."

Brandon turned toward his father. "Dad, I want you to meet Mandy. She's in one of my classes at the college."

The cold gray eyes of her rapist met hers from across the room. "Nice to meet you, Mandy."

So, he's going to play it like that, is he? Well, fuck you! I refuse to let you be in control of this. "Matt."

Brandon looked confused as his gaze went back and forth between her and his father. "Do you two know each other?"

"You could say that," she replied, taking Jonathan's hand in her own for strength. She needed his presence to keep her centered. "My mother is married to his brother."

"He's your uncle by marriage? Really. Wow. I never knew that." Brandon turned toward his father. "Uncle Roland is her stepfather?"

"Yes."

"Apparently, he didn't share a lot of things with you, Brandon." She laughed a dry, brittle sound. "He used to spend Christmases with us."

"That must have been when I was living with mom."

The man never took his gaze off her. Her skin crawled with revulsion. "I imagine so, Brandon." She wanted to shout to the heavens about how he'd forced himself on her and raped her in her own bedroom, but for some reason she kept quiet. Maybe she wanted him to acknowledge what he'd done to her, but she figured he never would. As far as he was concerned, he hadn't done anything wrong.

Matt lowered his gaze to the table, leaving her curious and apprehensive.

"I'm sorry, Mandy."

Her heart stopped beating. He hadn't just apologized, had he? No, it was a trick, an illusion. He wasn't sorry. He was repentant. He was the bastard who had taken everything from her and left her a hollow and broken person, someone who'd turned to drugs and prostitution to make herself feel like someone cared. Should she acknowledge his apology?

She looked at Jonathan.

Understanding swam in his gaze as he nodded without saying a word. He was leaving it up to her to decide what she should do, but he would support her in whatever that decision might be. She swallowed hard, the accusations hanging on the tip of her tongue.

When she glanced back at Matt, she saw something different. He was old and harried. Maybe what he'd done played hard on his soul. She hoped so, but she had to come to terms with either pressing charges against him for something that happened ten years ago or moving on with her life. Her life needed to revolve around finding her daughter, living with the man who had her heart in the palm of his hands, and who would keep her safe and love her no matter what.

"Jonathan, let's go."

"Are you sure, darlin'?"

"Yeah. I'm suddenly hungry for Mexican food rather than a burger."

"Whatever you want, honey."

They scooted out of the booth, leaving the two men to watch them leave never knowing how hard it was for her to walk away from her past and move on with her future.

When they reached the side of his truck on the passenger side, Jonathan leaned down and kissed her soundly on the mouth. "You did well, Mandy. I hope you know I will support you no matter what you decide to do. Personally, I would kick the man's ass for you, but it's your decision on how to handle things."

"I know, and I love you all the more for it. You're my rock, baby, and I will love you forever."

He helped her up inside the truck, buckled her seatbelt for her, and then shut the door behind him. Stopping in front of the vehicle, he turned toward where the two men were still watching through the windows. She saw him turn his right hip toward them, making sure they were aware of the pistol he carried in the holster. Matt went pale before turning back toward his son.

Jonathan went around to the driver's side, opened the door, and hopped in.

Once he'd started the truck, she took his hand in hers, lacing their fingers together before she brought it to her lips and kissed him on the back of the hand. "I love you."

He smiled at her before he checked around the truck and then backed out of the spot.

After they were seated at the Mexican restaurant, he asked, "Are you okay?"

"Yeah. Actually, I'm better than I've ever been. I have some closure now, and I'm ready to move on with my life. The situation is in my past, and I refuse to let it control me anymore."

"You probably should still get some counseling."

"I know and I will. I'll ask Peyton who she trusts and recommends." She brought their hands together on the tabletop. "I want you to know though that it's over. I'm a better person now, and I'm ready to make my life with you."

"I'm ready for us to build a life together."

"Me too."

He kissed her fingers as the waitress brought their menus. "What can I get you two to drink?"

"Coke for me."

"Me too."

"Coming right up."

When he finally let go of her hands, she opened her menu to decide what she wanted to eat. Enchiladas sounded really good, she decided, realizing her shoulders felt lighter now that she'd gotten rid of the weight she'd been carrying for such a long time. "Will you help me find my daughter?"

"Of course, honey. I know how important that is for you, but be prepared, she may not want anything to do with you."

"I know and that's something I'll have to deal with, but I want to tell her that I didn't give her up because I wanted to, I was forced to, and she's a part of me even if she chooses not to be a part of my life."

"We will start first thing in the morning. It might take a while to find her."

"It's okay. However long it takes."

"You should make a list of everything you know. Who the agency was you went through, her birthdate, what hospital she was born in, the doctor who delivered her, and so on. The more information you have, the easier it will be to get answers."

She smiled across the table at the man she loved. Leave it to him to prioritize everything so quickly and efficiently. They would find her. She just knew they would.

Epilogue

Mandy vibrated with excitement as they stood near the park bench at Concepcion Park. Jonathan stood next to her with his arm around her shoulders, holding her in one spot so she wouldn't float away on the cloud of happiness surrounding her.

She glanced down at the ring on her left hand sparkling in the summer sunshine. He'd given it to her the week after they had run into her rapist at the burger shop in Bandera, when he'd asked her to marry him. The wedding was planned for the fall at Thunder Ridge.

Today, she stood waiting for her daughter to arrive at the park so she could see her for the first time.

Miraculously enough, they had managed to track her down to where she lived with her parents in Houston, within two months of starting their search.

Thank God, for social media.

Mandy had contacted the attorney who'd worked with her parents on the adoption. He said he couldn't help her without contacting the parents who had adopted her daughter to make sure it was okay with them that he put her in touch with them. Luckily for her, they had agreed. The attorney had given Mandy their name and address, telling her they wanted her to write to them first before they agreed to tell her daughter about her.

Their first priority was the girl.

Mandy agreed. She didn't want to do anything that would hurt her daughter in any shape or form. If it was better for the girl to not know her, then so be it.

When the return letter had come back to her, she'd stared at it for two hours before she'd allowed herself to open it. Jonathan had been by her side, a rock in the storm of her life, while she fought with herself over whether this was the right thing to do.

After she'd finally tore it open and began to read, tears streamed down her face when she looked up and caught Jonathan's loving gaze with hers. "She wants to meet me."

"That's fantastic, darlin'."

She dropped the letter on the table and shook so hard, he had to take her in his arms to calm her down. "She wants to meet me, Jonathan. Oh my God! What will I say to her?"

"Tell her the truth, honey. You were only fifteen at the time and your parents didn't give you a choice."

"I know, but I'm afraid she'll hate me."

"I doubt she hates you, baby. She's coming from Houston to meet you. Are her parents coming too?"

"Yes. I think so."

Now, she stood here waiting with bated breath.

A black Chevrolet Capri pulled up to the curb near where they stood. No one moved.

Finally, the door opened and a beautiful young woman with bright red hair stepped out of the passenger side of the car, followed shortly by a nice looking man out of the driver's side. "Mandy?"

"Yes, ma'am."

"I'm Patricia Moore. This is my husband, Greg."

"It's nice to meet you."

"Gabriel is in the car. I told her to get out when she was ready."

"I appreciate you bringing her here."

"We were surprised by your correspondence with the attorney. We were not aware of the circumstances of her adoption until now. I'm very sorry about how things happened."

"It's okay. It wasn't your fault in any way. You wanted a child."

"Yes, we did, so very much, and she's been the bright spot in our lives for ten years."

Mandy held her breath as the door of the car slowly opened. A young girl with bright blonde hair stepped out, shutting the door behind her, before she slowly moved to her mother's side. At first she didn't even meet Mandy's gaze, but as she raised her head and looked at Mandy, Mandy's heart stopped in her chest. The same exact blue eyes that stared back at her in the mirror every day were gracing her daughter's face.

"Hi." Mandy stepped forward, but the little girl stepped back. "It's okay. I know you don't know me. My name is Mandy."

The little girl peeked around her mother's back, taking a long look at her before her gaze ricocheted to Jonathan. Mandy knew he could be intimidating with his size. "That's my fiancé. He won't hurt you, baby. His name is Jonathan."

"Are you really my mother?"

"I gave birth to you, yes, but Patricia is your mother. She's been with you since you were born."

Gabrielle's brows crinkled as she looked up at Patricia and then back at Mandy. "I don't understand."

"It's hard to explain, sweetie." Mandy held out her hand. "Can we sit down for a minute so I can explain?"

Gabrielle moved around Patricia and walked toward her although she didn't take Mandy's hand. She took a seat on the bench, her feet swinging back and forth.

"You see, when I had you in my stomach, I was only fifteen, and I couldn't take care of you like you deserved to be taken care of." Mandy wasn't about to go into the circumstances of how she got pregnant or why her parents made her give the little girl up, but she did want to explain as best she could. "Patricia and Greg wanted a child. When you were born, I let them take you so you could have a wonderful life with loving parents, a beautiful home, and be loved."

"Didn't you love me?"

"Oh, honey, more than anything in the world, but since I was so young myself, I couldn't take care of you even though I loved you so much, it made my heart hurt to let you go."

"Do you have other kids?"

"No."

"Why not?"

"Unfortunately, sweetie, I can't have any more babies."

Her face scrunched up as she looked at Mandy. "What do you want from me?"

"I just wanted to know you are happy and healthy. I wanted you to know I loved you then and I love you now, but I know you have your own life and I won't try to stick my nose into it. I will leave you alone now, but if you ever decide you want to be a part of my life, you are more than welcome to." Mandy turned toward Jonathan, taking his hand in her own as she smiled up into his gorgeous face. "Let's go home."

As she took a couple of steps away from the little girl she might not ever know, she heard a small little voice behind her say, "Can I call you and talk to you whenever I want?"

Mandy turned back toward Gabrielle. "Honey, you can call me anytime. I would love to hear about school, your friends, and what you've been doing. I promise, I'm not trying to take your mom's place. I just want to get to know you."

Gabrielle stepped forward and wrapped her arms around Mandy's waist.

Tears blurred her vision as she hugged her daughter closer and whispered a quick thank you to God for bringing her little girl to her.

When she glanced at Jonathan, she could have sworn there were tears in his eyes too as he kissed her on the forehead. "I love you."

"I love you too," she whispered back.

Her life was now complete. She would get to know her daughter, marry the man of her dreams in a few short months, and together they would live happily ever after, just like in the storybooks.

The End

About the Author

Sandy Sullivan is a romance author, who, when not writing, spends her time with her husband Shaun on their farm in middle Tennessee. She loves to ride her horses, play with their dogs and relax on the porch, enjoying the rolling hills of her home south of Nashville. Country music is a passion of hers and she loves to listen to it while she writes.

She is an avid reader of romance novels and enjoys reading Nora Roberts, Jude Deveraux and Susan Wiggs. Finding new authors and delving into something different helps feed the need for literature. A registered nurse by education, she loves to help people and spread the enjoyment of romance to those around her with her novels. She loves cowboys so you'll find many of her novels have sexy men in tight jeans and cowboy boots.

Sandy's website
www.romancestorytime.com

Other books by Sandy

Love Me Once, Love Me Twice (Montana Cowboys 1)
Before the Night is Over (Montana Cowboys 2)
Two for the Price of One (Montana Cowboys 3)
Difficult Choices (Montana Cowboys 4)
Doctor Me Up (Montana Cowboys 5)
Stakin' His Claim
Country Minded Cougar
Meet Me in the Barn
Taming the Cougar
Trouble With a Cowboy
Gotta Love a Cowboy
Make Mine a Cowboy (Cowboy Dreamin' 1)
Healing a Cowboy's Heart (Cowboy Dreamin' 2)
For the Love of a Cowboy (Cowboy Dreamin' 3)
Tempted by the Cowboy (Cowboy Dreamin' 4)
Forever Kind of Cowboy (Cowboy Dreamin' 5)
Kiss Me, Cowboy (Cowboy Dreamin' 6)
A Cowboy and a Country Song (Cowboy Dreamin' 7)
Falling Hard (Eight Second Ride Book 1)
Loving Hard (Eight Second Ride Book 2)